SECRET SISTER

Sophie McKenzie

SIMON &
SCHUSTER

First published in Great Britain in 2023 by Simon & Schuster UK Ltd

Text copyright © 2023 Sophie McKenzie

1 3 5 7 9 10 8 6 4 2

Simon & Schuster UK Ltd
1st Floor, 222 Gray's Inn Road
London WC1X 8HB

www.simonandschuster.co.uk
www.simonandschuster.com.au
www.simonandschuster.co.in

Simon & Schuster Australia, Sydney
Simon & Schuster India, New Delhi

A CIP catalogue record for this book is available from the British Library.

PB ISBN 978-1-3985-2326-5
eBook ISBN 978-1-3985-2327-2
eAudio ISBN 978-1-3985-2328-9

Printed and Bound in the UK
using 100% Renewable Electricity
at CPI Group (UK) Ltd

MIX
Paper | Supporting
responsible forestry
FSC® C171272
FSC
www.fsc.org

For Kate Elliott

WILLOW

It's the second time I've had the feeling in as many hours . . .

Someone is watching me.

A shiver runs down my spine as I peer through the living-room window. The earlier drizzle has stopped, but the pavement outside still glistens with rain. I stare at the hedge that runs along the side of our front yard. I have this horrible sense someone is lurking among the dark, gleaming leaves.

Which is ridiculous.

There's nobody there.

I shift my gaze to my reflection in the window. Even in the haze of the glass, I can tell that my arms are too angular, sticking awkwardly out of my blue top. I don't really like this top, but one of the cool boys at school once said it was the same colour as my eyes, so maybe it suits me more than I think. I peer more closely at the glass and sigh, smoothing back a strand of fine, frizzy hair.

'Willow! Ah, there you are!' Dad calls from the

doorway. 'Can you help me with my work email? My phone seems to have locked me out.'

'Again?' I make a face, then follow him into the kitchen. Dad is the most un-techy man in the world. He's a financial adviser, and when he had to start using video calls during the pandemic, I honestly thought he might have to give up work, he found it so stressful. But he kept going and he's actually quite good at IT stuff now. He still says he can't be doing with most social media, but he does use old things like Facebook and sometimes posts pictures on Instagram.

The kitchen table is a huge wooden oblong that takes up one half of the room. Despite its size, it's constantly cluttered with Dad's books and the boys' games and toys. Right now, for instance, Dad's laptop is squished at one end of the table, next to a stack of files, while a gazillion plastic robots are scattered across the rest. My stepbrothers, Ben and Billy, are sitting on either side of the table. Quiet, geeky Ben is building yet another plastic robot while little Billy – who loves winding up his older brother – is making '*vroom, vroom*' noises as he drives a dented toy car across the table, scattering the bits Ben needs as he does so.

'Stop it, Billy!' Ben shouts. 'You're spoiling my robot.'

'*My* robot!' Billy shrieks, grinning from ear to ear.

I suppress a smile. Even when Billy's being super annoying, that cheeky grin of his makes it impossible to dislike him. I prod his arm. 'You know it isn't yours, Billy.'

'Is *too!*' insists Billy. He drives his car into a pile of purple plastic pieces, which promptly skitter across the table and cascade onto the floor.

'Hey!' Ben yells. 'You're ruining it!'

Dad looks up and frowns. 'Boys, please keep it down,' he says helplessly.

He's not the best at discipline. I think it's partly that my stepmum, Becky, is so good at it and partly because Dad's always been careful not to overstep. He's not the boys' biological dad, you see. Just mine. My mum – and my twin sister – were in a car crash and died just before my second birthday. Becky met Dad and came to live with us seven years ago, when Billy was one and Ben three.

I sit down next to Dad and take his phone. He frowns at his laptop while I tap at the phone screen and get Dad back into his work email. I glance over at the boys. Ben has picked up his robot pieces and is guarding them with his arm, while Billy looks on. Dad is engrossed in whatever he's reading on his laptop.

Nobody is watching me. I open the locator app on Dad's phone, which I know keeps tabs on my movements – or, rather, those of my mobile. It's the only thing Dad and

I argue about. I've given in on all the other things he's protective about: him picking me up from everywhere and speaking to parents if I'm staying over at a friend's house.

I think being able to track where I go takes the protective thing too far, especially now I'm almost fourteen. I know Becky agrees, but Dad refuses to give up the tracker. 'Maybe next year, Willow,' he says, whenever I ask. 'I only use it if you're out at a party.'

I carefully remove the track-phone function so Dad will no longer be able to follow my movements. If he's telling the truth about only using it when I'm at a party, he probably won't even notice for weeks.

As I put the phone back on the table, the front door slams shut.

'Mum!' Billy yells. 'Ben won't let me play with his robots!'

'Because you break them!' Ben's voice rises with hurt anger. 'You—!'

'That's enough, boys.' Becky sweeps into the kitchen, her red hair tied back in a messy bun. She dumps her shopping bag on the nearest free chair. 'Your turn to help me unload, Billy.'

If Dad had asked, Billy would undoubtedly have made a fuss, but he knows better than to fight his mum over household chores. Becky might be tiny – I overtook her

4

height-wise last year – but she's fierce.

'I'm not bringing up a pair of useless boys who expect a woman to run around after them,' she often says.

Billy hoists a loaf of bread out of the shopping bag while Becky fills the kettle. Dad, after catching her hand and squeezing it as she passes, is poring over his laptop again. I get up and fetch the tin of teabags down from the shelf.

'I'll make it,' I say, popping three bags in the big stainless-steel teapot.

Becky throws me a grateful smile. 'Thanks, love,' she says. 'Hey, Willow, you still haven't said what you want to do for your birthday? Takeaway? Meal out somewhere special? Pizza and a few friends?'

I shrug, feeling awkward. My fourteenth birthday is on Wednesday and, so far, I've resisted all attempts to organize any kind of celebration. I ruled out a party weeks ago. I definitely don't want to be the centre of attention. The thought of opening presents with my friends focused on my reactions is beyond horrifying.

'We can organize whatever you like,' Becky says. 'No noisy sleepover though, as it's a school night.'

'Would you like to see some of your mum's family?' Dad asks gently. 'I'm sure they'd love to see you on your birthday.'

'I guess.' I don't really know my aunts and uncles from

my birth mother's side of the family very well, so the idea of meeting up isn't that appealing. On the other hand, I do have two cousins my age, and the last time I saw them we got on great.

'It's a fantastic idea to invite them over, but it's a long way for them to come on a weeknight,' ever-practical Becky points out. 'Maybe we could organize a lunch party for next weekend?' she suggests.

'Okay,' I say.

'Of course, that still leaves your actual birthday on Wednesday,' Becky goes on.

Dad gazes at me, eyes full of sadness. 'That would have also been . . .' He looks away, clearly thinking about my twin sister.

I stare at him, feeling awkward. Dad and I used to talk about my mum and sister a lot, but recently I've become aware that whereas Dad still misses them, it's different for me. Sometimes I feel the *lack* of them, but you can't miss what you don't remember.

'Oh, Billy, no!' Becky sighs.

We all follow her gaze to where Billy is attempting to refill the sugar canister from the new bag Becky just brought in with the shopping. Tiny white sprinkles of sugar are spilling out across the countertop and onto the floor.

As Becky and Dad leap into action, the kettle comes to

the boil. I pour water into the teapot, then slip out into the back garden. The sun is out now, so I brush the rain off the plastic swing seat and plonk myself down.

It's not that I don't want a party. It's that parties mean photos and videos and social media and everyone at school judging you. If I had fuller lips and thicker hair and didn't look so shapeless, I wouldn't mind having a big get-together with everyone I know invited and taking a million photos. In fact, I'd love it.

I push myself back, then let the seat go. As I swing forward, I get that feeling of being watched again. I stop the swing and look over to the fence that borders the side street – our house is on the corner.

There! I catch a flash of blue between the fence posts. My breath catches in my throat. Was that just someone walking past?

Or is someone out there, lurking?

I tiptoe to the gate in the fence and ease it silently open. My heart is beating hard as I peer up and down the pavement. For a second I think the street is empty; then a boy in a blue hoodie steps out from behind a van parked a short way down the road. He walks towards me. I'm frozen to the spot.

The boy looks a little older than I am, with dark wavy hair, high cheekbones and piercing blue eyes. Even as the

7

fear rises inside me, I notice that he is strikingly handsome.

He stops walking. We stare at each other. My heart races.

'Willow?' he asks. His voice is low and very, very serious.

I nod, too shocked to speak.

'I wasn't sure whether to knock on the door,' he says, a crooked smile flitting across his face. 'But I wanted to get you on your own.'

These words should turn my fear into outright panic, but the boy doesn't look like he wants to hurt me. If anything, he seems nervous. His hands pick at the strap of his backpack.

'What do you want?' I croak.

The boy hesitates. 'I've got a message,' he says. 'A message from your twin sister.'

'From . . . from . . . ?' I shake my head and take a step away. Whoever this boy is, he's clearly either crazy or deliberately trying to upset me.

'Please,' he urges. 'Don't go – I'm serious. I'm sure you know that a body was never found and . . . I know it must sound mad, but . .'

'My sister is dead.' My voice is ice cold.

'No, she's alive,' the boy says. 'Asha's alive.'

TWO WEEKS EARLIER

ASHA

The daily roster of people to help the Ricketts' deal with this week's lambing is decided and Lydia calls the weekly island meeting to order.

'Right,' she says briskly. 'That's the end of the formal agenda. Time for any other business, but small items only, please. Anything requiring a debate needs to be tabled for proper discussion next week.'

The residents of Dimity Island glance at each other, clearly wondering if anyone has an issue to raise. There are twenty-four people in our commune at the moment and, apart from the very littlest children who are doing a puzzle in the corner of the room, we are all sitting around the big table in the Community Room. The sun is shining through the long windows at the end of the room. Lydia stands at the head of the table, eyebrows raised expectantly.

'Well, if there isn't any—'

'Er, I was wondering if we could have a potluck at the end of the month?' Mum says, blushing furiously next to me. 'For . . . for Asha's birthday. And the spring equinox.'

She hates speaking in front of people. It's a sign of how much she wants to make my birthday special that she's raising the subject at all.

I smile at her.

'A potluck party,' Lydia muses, peering at me over her glasses. 'Remind me, how old will you be, Asha?'

'Fourteen,' I say. 'I'll be fourteen on the twenty-second.'

A murmur ripples round the table.

Tem, Lydia's husband, gives a chuckle. 'Wow, Rose, that must mean it's twelve years since you and Asha arrived here,' he says.

Mum nods. 'To the day, actually.'

'Happy anniversary!' cries Tem, who is as round and jolly as Lydia is slender and sharp. Others around the table murmur: 'Where does the time go!' and 'I can't believe it's so long!' Wrinkly-faced Sally Brickman, sitting on the other side of me from Mum, pats me on the shoulder.

I resist the temptation to roll my eyes. Older people talk about time like it's a shooting star, zipping past them at the speed of light. To me, time passes slowly.

Agonizingly slowly.

Don't get me wrong. I love how we live here on Dimity Island, but every day is the same and, sometimes, it really drags. Meanwhile there's a whole world, out on the mainland and beyond, that I've only ever read about in books.

Only one person on the island really understands how frustrating that is – Silas. I glance across the table at him. He's looking down at his lap, frowning – as he has been the whole meeting.

Lydia clears her throat and the room quietens. 'I think a potluck for the spring equinox is a marvellous idea. We can incorporate all the spring birthdays into the celebration, including yours, Asha.' She beams at me, then glances around the table. 'Let's schedule it for the last Saturday of March, that's the twenty-fifth, at 8 p.m.?'

No one disagrees, so Lydia makes a note on her clipboard, then peers over at Mum and her friend and fellow baker, Annie. 'Will you two handle the decorations?'

'Course,' Annie says.

'Oh, thank you, Lydia,' Mum says. Her hands fly to the silver crescent moon around her neck. As she fiddles with the necklace, she absently flicks her hair over her shoulders. It flutters down her back, like waves of feathery golden barley. With my dark hair and eyes, I don't look anything like her. This isn't surprising. My biological mother was called Jasmine Hope. She died when her car skidded off a cliff road and crashed onto the rocks below. Somehow, I survived and, as Jasmine was a single mum

13

with no family, Mum – who can't have kids herself – adopted me. She always says I'm her miracle baby. Lydia helped Mum bring me to the island, where we've lived ever since. Most people visit the mainland from time to time, to see friends and family, but Mum says she's happy to leave her old life behind; that now her own parents have passed away, we've got no reason to ever go back.

'Well, if that's all?' Lydia looks around the table.

'Actually, I have a question.' Silas stands up.

I bite my lip, wondering what he's going to ask. Silas has a habit of challenging Lydia and Tem – saying the things that I only dare to think. Mum says he's just 'at that age'. But I don't think being almost sixteen automatically makes you a rebel. He's certainly the most interesting – and attractive – boy who lives here. It's not just the sea-blue colour of his eyes or the square-jawed lines of his face; it's something on the inside too. Something that makes Silas different. Special.

Special to me, anyway. Not that anyone knows how I feel.

'What is it now, Silas?' Lydia asks, an edge to her voice.

Silas leans forward and his fringe tumbles over his eyes. My heart gives a little bump.

'I want a mobile phone,' he says. 'Why can't I get one? It's ridiculous that you've banned them and—'

14

'Come on, Silas, we haven't *banned* anything,' Tem interrupts. 'The whole commune took a vote and *chose* to avoid personal electronic devices.'

'*I'm* banned from having one.' Silas glares at him.

Lydia tuts. 'That's because your parents left you in our care while they're away. They are as against electronic devices as the rest of us. They aren't compatible with the traditional way we live, or the pace of life we believe makes us healthy.'

'But—' Silas starts.

'It's not like we're living in the dark ages,' Lydia interrupts. 'As you well know, there's an emergency mobile phone and a computer in our apartment. Anyone on the island is free to use those to make contact with friends and relatives on the mainland whenever they want.' She sniffs, clearly irritated.

I look at Silas, willing him to argue back. Beside me, Mum is twisting her hands together. She hates it when there's any conflict.

'Emergency phone calls and five minutes every now and then on a basic PC aren't enough,' Silas snaps. 'Not for me. What about social media? Or the internet?'

A shivery thrill runs down my spine as the room falls into a tense silence. I don't know much about either of those things Silas has mentioned, but I know that most people on Dimity Island consider them highly dangerous, especially for young people whose lives can be dominated – and ruined – by them.

The whole point about life on the island is to live in harmony with nature, avoiding – as Tem says *very* often – the destructive technologies and the political-military-industrial complex that corrupts life elsewhere. A boat comes every other Friday to top up our supplies, but otherwise we farm sheep and grow small amounts of crops and live quietly and sustainably in our cottages.

Lydia shakes her head. 'This isn't up for discussion, Silas. You can use our phone to talk to your parents whenever you want. That's the best we can do.' She sighs, heavily.

I watch Silas, his expressive face churning with fury. Mum has told me several times recently that Lydia and Tem have been struggling to deal with him. His parents – both doctors, who moved to the island when Silas was seven – went away at the start of the year on a five-month work trip to Eritrea. There was a big debate about whether Silas and his sister, Pixie, should be left on their own while their parents were gone. Silas swayed the argument by saying that he was almost sixteen and would be leaving for sixth form on the mainland in September anyway, while Pixie was already fourteen. He agreed that Tem and Lydia would act as his guardians – and pointed out that there were plenty of people just minutes away if they needed help.

'This place is such a dictatorship,' Silas spits.

The atmosphere tenses again – he's gone too far now. Tem and Lydia might own the island, but we have weekly meetings to decide how everything – from the harvests to the baking rotas – are run. And everyone gets a say at these. I glance at Lydia. The tiny muscle in her temple is twitching, which means she is super furious. She's not the only one. Winston Rickett – who co-manages the sheep farm – mutters something angrily to his wife, Chola. Across the table, our resident vet, Samira Asiki, rolls her eyes, while Max, our school teacher, shakes his head wearily. He's used to Silas's outbursts.

Lydia opens her mouth, but before she can speak, Silas points his finger at her. 'You,' he says, 'are a fascist who shouldn't be running a bath, let alone a community of people.'

Gasps run round the table. Tem leaps up. 'That's enough!' he growls.

'You're grounded, Silas,' Lydia snaps. 'Nothing but school and chores for the next month.'

'That's all there is to do here anyway,' Silas snaps back.

'Is that so?' Lydia's eyes narrow. 'Well, you will *definitely* be missing the potluck party.'

'Oh no, *please*——!' The words escape out of me before I can stop them.

Everyone looks at me. I feel the heat of their gaze, my own cheeks burning. Beside me, Mum is frowning with concern. Opposite me, Pixie's mouth has fallen open. I sneak a tiny look sideways at Silas, who seems surprised.

They've all seen. Now everyone knows how much I like him.

I jump up and push my chair back, then race out of the Community Room. Behind me I can hear Lydia telling Mum to let me be. I tear across the hall, out of the front door and into the bright sunshine.

How could I have given myself away like that?

I race along the path in the direction of home. Just before I reach our cottage, I turn up Oak Tree Hill.

The higher I get, the more fiercely the March wind whips across my face. I stand at the top and gaze along the island, gleaming green in the sun. If it were a finger, you could say where I'm standing is at the middle knuckle. From here I can see all three miles to the northern end, though the southern tip and Dimity House itself are hidden by a curve in the land – as if the pointy bit of the finger is slightly bent to the left.

I sink down onto the grass. The wind is seriously

gusting and I'm freezing cold, even in the bright sunshine. I squeeze my eyes tight shut, wishing I could make the last few minutes go away. The gentle rustle of grass tells me footsteps are approaching. I open my eyes, expecting to see Mum. Or perhaps Pixie. She's pretty much my best friend on the island and, I'm sure, had no idea until just now what a massive crush I have on her brother.

Instead, it's Silas himself who is standing in front of me.

'Hi.' I meet his gaze, my insides squirming.

'Hi,' he says, squatting down.

He's going to say something about my feelings for him . . . I'm certain he is. Something totally embarrassing like he's sorry I'm so into him, but I'm just a kid, a part of the life he's desperate to leave behind. But instead he grins and says, 'Thanks for supporting me in there.'

I look up. Shrug, feeling relieved. Perhaps my feelings weren't as obvious as I'd thought. 'No problem,' I say.

'I was wondering . . .' Silas hesitates. 'Can you keep a secret?'

'Sure.' I sit up straighter. 'Go on.'

'I've decided to leave the island,' he says. 'I'd be going in the autumn anyway, but I can't wait.'

'Run away? Seriously?' It's not a shock to me that Silas wants to go; just surprising that he thinks it's possible.

There's only one way off the island – by sea – and only two boats that ever come anywhere near it: the cabin cruiser from Salthaven that drops off our fortnightly supplies; and Lydia and Tem's motorboat, which is moored a little way along from Dimity House in a small boat shelter. 'I get why you want to go, but . . . but *how*?'

'I'm going to steal Lydia and Tem's boat,' Silas says. 'It's the only way.'

'But . . . but what about your parents?' I stammer. 'What about Pixie?'

Silas shrugs. 'Mum and Dad aren't due home for three months, so—'

'Can't you wait for them, at least?'

'No,' he says. 'I *have* to get away from here before I go mad.' He sighs. 'I hate leaving Pixie, but your mum will look after her – they're really close.' He leans forward, a strand of dark hair falling over those intense sea-blue eyes. 'You'll take care of her too, won't you?'

My stomach gives another funny flip. 'Sure,' I say.

'I'm going to look for the key to the boat tomorrow, while Lydia and Tem are helping with the lambing.' Silas hesitates. 'I know it's a lot to ask, but I can see that you understand how I feel from the way you acted just now, when Lydia was having a go at me.' He pauses again. 'So . . . will you keep lookout for me while I search their apartment?'

I gulp. It's a scary prospect, but there's no way I can turn Silas down.

'Sure,' I say. 'Of course I will.'

The evening passes slowly. Mum brings home scones from the baking she did after the community meeting and – after I've reassured her that I only ran off earlier because I was embarrassed everyone was looking at me – we eat them with home-made butter and thick dollops of Sally Brickman's strawberry jam. Well, Mum does. To be honest, I'm so nervous about keeping lookout for Silas tomorrow that everything tastes like dust and cardboard.

How on earth does Silas think he'll find the key to Lydia and Tem's boat? I have no idea where they keep it. What if we're caught snooping in their flat? I want to help Silas, but I'm scared. Unlike him, I'm used to following the rules and doing what I'm told.

Mum doesn't seem to notice how preoccupied I am. She nibbles on her scone and chatters away about the party at the end of the month.

'I think I'll wear my teal skirt,' she says, 'and that bracelet Lydia gave me. Gosh, it's so kind of her to agree to the party.'

I don't say it out loud, but I don't really think that

kindness has much to do with it. Lydia wasn't that bothered about having a party either way – though I'm certain that if she hadn't wanted one, it wouldn't be happening. I might not go as far as Silas in saying that she runs the island like a dictator, but she certainly exerts a massive amount of influence on everything that happens here.

'What do you think *you'll* wear, Asha?' Mum asks.

I shrug – clothes are the last thing on my mind – then pour us both another cup of tea. I put the milk and the butter back in the fridge. We have wind turbines at the northerly tip of the island, which provide electricity on a generator. It means everyone can keep things cool in fridges, so we waste less food, and it allows the lights to come on in the evening for a few hours too. I know that on the mainland, they use electricity *all* the time. It's so extravagant and bad for the environment. According to Tem, office buildings even keep their lights on through the night!

'Perhaps Pixie will have something she can lend you,' Mum suggests.

'What?' I stare at her.

'For you to wear . . .' Mum frowns. 'To the party.'

'Oh.' It suddenly strikes me that if Silas is successful in his bid to escape from the island tomorrow, he won't be here for the party. In fact, I might not ever see him again.

22

The thought is horrible.

'Mum?' I say. 'Why don't we ever leave the island?'

Mum frowns, clearly surprised that I'm asking.

'We've talked about this,' she says gently. 'The mainland is a corrupt and polluted environment full of bad and dangerous people. There's nothing for us there.'

'But everyone else goes,' I point out. 'The Asikis all went for three weeks over Christmas to see family, and they survived it all right. And when Aaron Brickman went to uni, he came back with Eva, and now they have two kids, so—'

'Well, I want more for you than just "survival". And there's plenty of time for exploring what you want to be.' Mum tuts. 'Please, Asha, I know it's important that we're open to newcomers so long as they share our values.' She smiles. I don't smile back. 'But it's different for us. You and me. We don't have any family to go back to.'

I fall silent. I am, of course, only too aware of this. When I was little I used to ask, over and over again, for Mum to tell me how she came to adopt me. It's an amazing story. She actually rescued me from the car crash that killed my biological mother. It happened near a place called Bridmouth, on the mainland coast. Apparently I was in my baby seat and thrown free from the car onto some rocks. Mum was passing and saw me – and the tide

23

coming in – and she scrambled down the rocks to save me in the nick of time.

'We just have each other,' Mum says gently. 'You and me. And everyone else on the island is all the family we need. People who have pledged to live by the four *T*s.' She's referring to the island's four founding principles: truth, tolerance, transparency and trust. 'You know, Asha, those things are in short supply in the outside world.'

I think of Silas, so eager to get away and explore that world. 'What if I want to leave some day?'

'Well, there's plenty of time to talk about that. No point discussing it now.' She stands up. 'Come on, we need to water and feed the hens before bed.'

And, before I can ask any more, she leaves the cottage.

The next morning brings a steel-grey sky with a definite threat of rain. It's as gloomy as yesterday was crisp and sunny. All I can think about is that soon I'll be keeping a lookout for Silas while he snoops around Lydia and Tem's apartment. I trudge into the kitchen, feeling nervous. Mum's cheery 'hello' grates on my ears. She starts chatting about the day's planting – onions and beets – and how we're spending the morning at the Ricketts' cottage looking after the baby and cooking meals for the day, while the rest of the family – plus Samira, Lydia and Tem – help with the lambing.

I listen in silence, fetching a bowl of porridge from the pot on the hob, then cooling it with cream from the island dairy and sprinkling it with pumpkin seeds from our very own patch.

Mum is still chattering away as we walk across the island to the Ricketts' cottage. The wind whips around us, fierce in our faces, and the clouds hang heavily overhead: dark and ominous. There's no rain yet though and no sign of anyone out in Cass Field: just twenty or so sheep – and a few new lambs – nibbling at the grass. As we watch, Tem and Lydia come into view, heading towards the lambing barn. Tem lopes along, a big bear of a man, while Lydia strides purposefully, all tightly controlled sharp angles.

'I expect Winston's already up to his ears,' Mum says, picking up the pace.

We meet Chola Rickett as she hurries out of her front door, her grubby overall buttoned the wrong way.

'Got to dash,' she says, smiling as she squeezes Mum's arm with her large, rough hands. She points back to the house. 'The baby's in her pram in the backyard. She needs to come in for a nap before it rains.'

'Don't worry about anything, Cho,' Mum says. 'Asha and I have got it covered.'

'Thanks.' Chola runs off, taking huge strides in her hefty farm boots.

Mum and I head indoors. The Ricketts' cottage is only slightly larger than ours and overflowing, as usual, with clutter. Mum sends me to fetch and settle the baby. Of course, she cries when I try to put her down, so I hold her, rocking her in front of the mirror. In just a few minutes' time, I'm going to have to make an excuse and leave. I stare at my reflection. My eyes are wide and frightened-looking.

I put the baby in her cot again, and this time, thankfully, she stops fussing and falls asleep.

It's time for me to leave. I head to the kitchen, where Mum is surrounded by pots and pans, making a huge tureen of vegetable soup. I take the milk pail from the fridge and peer inside. It's actually almost half full, but I tell Mum it's empty, forcing myself to look her in the eye as I do so. 'Shall I take it up to the Big House and refill it?' I ask. My cheeks feel hot – I'm sure that my face must be giving me away.

'Okay.' Mum nods, distractedly. 'I'll keep an eye on the baby,' she says, 'but don't be too long. I want to give the place a proper spring clean.' She smiles.

I smile back, feeling suddenly guilty. *It's so easy to lie when people trust you.*

I pick up the milk pail and hurry outside. The sky is even darker than when we arrived, the air now heavy with the coming rain. I scuttle along the path, skirting around the base of Oak Tree Hill, then crossing Polaris Field. Silas meets me, as arranged, just past his and Pixie's cottage.

'You're here,' he says, giving me that smile that makes my stomach cartwheel.

I nod, feeling awkward. The wind whips across our faces. My long hair is tied back, but a strand comes free and flies into my eyes. I brush it away as the first few spots of rain land on my cheek.

Silas pulls up the hood of his jacket. 'Let's go,' he says.

We cut across Orion Field, where the island's two horses, Marx and Engels, raise their heads as they sniff our scent – then follow the sloping land down to the south-eastern tip of the island. A few minutes later we round the bend in the path and Dimity House comes into view.

'I know Tem and Lydia aren't here,' I say, 'but how do you know the house is empty?'

'I don't.' Silas's eyes sparkle with excitement. 'But if anyone's there, they'll be downstairs, not up in Tem and Lydia's apartment. Come on.'

Despite the uneasy feeling uncoiling inside me, I follow him around the side of the house. I leave the milk

27

pail on the grass and we slip inside via the side door to the senior schoolroom. The door is, of course, unlocked. Nobody locks doors here – what would anyone steal? Part of living as a community means that although we have our individual spaces and possessions, nobody really owns anything valuable. Everybody contributes what they can and trusts everyone else to do the same.

'This is such a big house,' Silas mutters as we tiptoe across the senior schoolroom. 'Does that seem right to you? That Tem and Lydia have so much space, while families like the Ricketts' are crammed into tiny cottages?'

I frown. I've never really thought about it like that. Mum has always described Tem and Lydia as super generous. Apparently, when Tem's parents bought the island back in the 1970s, they charged other residents rent, but that stopped when Tem and Lydia took over. Now everything operates like a commune, with nobody better off than anyone else.

'We all use the ground floor,' I point out. 'So you can't say that Tem and Lydia really have the whole house for themselves.'

'They do when nobody else is here,' Silas says with a grunt.

I glance around the deserted senior schoolroom. It's weird being here at the weekend, when the desks are empty and the room so silent. Monday's Maths test is almost certainly in Max – the teacher's – desk drawer. For a second I'm tempted to sneak a peek; then I push the urge away and join Silas beside the door that leads into the hall.

At first there's no sound coming from the other side. But, as Silas gently twists the handle and starts to open the door, footsteps echo across the hall's wooden floor.

Silas and I freeze. Who is out there?

'Lydia?' It's Mum's friend Annie. 'I thought you were at the Ricketts' this morning?'

Silas and I stare at each other in horror.

I peer through the crack between the schoolroom door and its frame. Lydia is striding across the hall towards the kitchen. Annie is standing in the kitchen doorway, wiping her floury hands on her apron.

'I'm not needed for the lambing after all, so I've come back to . . .' The rest of Lydia's sentence is lost as she disappears after Annie into the kitchen.

Silas and I stare at each other.

'Should we turn back?' I whisper.

'No.' Silas frowns. 'No, it's Sunday. There'll be far more people here during the week. If we don't go now, there won't be a better chance until next weekend. I can't wait.'

'Okay.' I nod, trying to steady my nerves. 'But suppose Lydia goes up to her flat?'

'We'll just have to take that chance. I'll be quick.' Silas hesitates. 'You don't have to do this, Asha.'

'No,' I say. 'Let's go.' To show I mean what I say, I slip past him and into the hall. I creep silently across the wooden floorboards and up the stairs, Silas right behind me.

The top step groans as I land on it.

My heart races. Did anyone hear?

Nobody appears.

'So far, so good,' Silas whispers. His breathing is rapid and shallow. He might look calm on the outside, but I reckon he's as nervous as I am. 'You wait here – let me know if anyone comes into the hall. If they see you up here, you can just pretend we were looking for Lydia.'

I give Silas a nod of agreement, then look around the landing. Tem and Lydia's open-plan living-and-kitchen area is visible through the open doors opposite. With Silas's earlier words still in my head, I notice how huge it really is. 'Where do you think the key is?' I whisper.

'I'm going to try in here first.' Silas slips through the first doorway on the left, into Lydia and Tem's study.

I shuffle closer to the doorway, still keeping my gaze on the stairs. A shiver wriggles down my spine. Silas might be used to rebelling, but I've never done anything remotely like this before.

I glance into the study. It's crammed and cluttered with paperwork, piles of which are spread out over much of the carpeted floor. Shelves heaving with files and folders run from floor to ceiling all the way along one wall. Two desks sit at right angles to each other, one in front of each of the room's two windows. There's a filing cabinet beside the larger, tidier desk – and a big cupboard in the alcove in the corner.

Silas is making his way methodically around the room, examining each drawer and shelf as he goes. A stray curl of dark hair falls over his eyes as he bends over the contents of the tidier leather-topped desk. Lydia's. A small vase of snowdrops stands next to the computer terminal.

Silas must sense me watching him because he looks up and grimaces. 'You know Lydia has an iPad in here. So much for "emergency calls only".'

'Any sign of the boat key?' I ask.

Silas shakes his head. 'The only key I've found is this.' He holds up a rusty, old-fashioned key with a long blade. 'It was right at the back of this drawer. I don't know what it's for, but there's no way it has anything to do with the motorboat.' He lays it down on the desk top and keeps searching.

I check the time – it feels much longer, but Silas has only been in the study for ten minutes. I tiptoe across the landing and look properly down the stairs. There's no sign of anyone in the hall and no sounds coming from the kitchen beyond. Perhaps Lydia got whatever she was looking for and has already left again.

Still, we shouldn't hang around.

I go back to the study. Silas has moved on to the second desk – Tem's – and is rifling through the top drawer. He glances up at me.

'This is *so* messy,' he grumbles. 'It's going to take me ages to check through everything.'

'Let me help,' I say, hurrying into the room. 'I think Lydia must have gone – there's no sign of her downstairs.'

Silas nods. 'Okay, why don't you check in there?' He points to the enormous wooden cupboard in the alcove in the corner. It's as high as my shoulders and twice as deep as any of our cupboards at home.

I nod and scuttle over. I tug at the door.

'It's locked,' I hiss.

Silas points to the rusty key still lying on the desktop. 'Try that.'

I take the key and insert it into the lock. It takes a bit of effort, but the door swings open. I grin to myself and peer into the huge cupboard.

A single shelf runs along the middle, splitting the cupboard in half. Both top and bottom are piled with folders and files and random bits of paper. I am just about to pull out some of the paperwork, when the top step of the stairs gives a loud creak. Someone is coming!

My stomach plummets. Silas's head shoots up. '*Hide!*' he mouths.

There's no time to think. I shove aside the files in the bottom left of the cupboard and hurl myself into the space created. There's just room for me to crouch down. Reaching for the door, I curl my fingertips around the edge to pull it shut. It almost closes. Through the gap I can make out Silas, hunched over his knees, under Tem's desk.

It's dark and dusty in here, only a tiny streak of light filtering in from the gap.

I barely dare breath as the footsteps draw closer.

Tap, tap on the landing; then a quieter *pad, pad* as whoever it is moves onto the carpet of the study. I peer through the crack again.

Please don't be Lydia.

But it is. A moment later her white trainers pace back and forth past my hiding place. My blood is like ice in my veins. Lydia stops in the middle of the room and turns slowly round. I can only see her from the knees down. I hold my breath. Seconds later she walks out of sight. I wait to hear her footsteps out on the landing, but the sound doesn't come. She must still be in the room.

The need to sneeze from all the dust builds inside

me. I turn my head, lift my hand, slowly, and pinch my nose hard. I'm adjusting to the dim light in here now and sit, swallowing down the desire to sneeze. My heart is thumping so loud, surely Lydia will hear it. My eyes water.

Pad, pad.

Lydia's feet appear again through the crack in the door. She's close to me now. Bending down. Her hand reaches for the door. I hold myself still. Rigid. Any second, she'll open the door and find me. I squeeze my eyes tight shut.

'Are you looking for me?' It's Silas.

My eyes shoot open. Through the crack I see Lydia spin round and straighten up. Silas is walking out from his hiding place.

'What are you doing in here?' Lydia demands.

'Trying to find a way off this stupid fascist island,' Silas snarls.

'How dare you!' Lydia's voice rises to a yell. She grabs Silas's arm.

He wrenches it away. 'Get off me.'

I watch them, my heart in my mouth.

'This is the last straw!' Lydia lunges again, but Silas dodges past her and she trips, knocking her head against a bookshelf. Rubbing her forehead, she turns and hurries after Silas. I can hear their footsteps out on the landing.

'Come back here!' Lydia shrieks. 'You're going to pay for this!'

A stream of swear words from Silas and more yells from Lydia. Other voices joining in now, a hubbub rising as they head down the stairs.

I stay where I am, curled up in the cupboard.

I'm still terrified, but also overjoyed.

And not just because I have escaped Lydia's fury.

But because Silas just gave himself away to save me.

I stay in the cupboard for two whole minutes, forcing myself to count the seconds under my breath. At last, I ease open the cupboard door and creep out, into the study. My body is cramped and sore. I stretch it out quickly, then turn back to the cupboard, trying to put the papers I moved back in their original positions.

As I shove a bundle of files aside, a photo falls out of a faded brown envelope. It's a picture of two toddlers sitting side by side on a rug. I peer more closely. The dark-haired little girl is me, I think, though the bright pink dress I'm wearing is like nothing I've ever seen myself in before. Is the other girl in the picture Pixie? She's the only person on the island close enough to my age. No, it can't be her – Pixie and Silas's family didn't arrive here until I was five years old.

There's no time to think about it now. I pocket the photo, relock the cupboard and tiptoe to the door. Silence from the ground floor. I wait another few seconds, then make my way downstairs as quietly as I can and into the senior schoolroom. I pick up the Ricketts' milk pail from the spot where I left it outside, then let out a long, shaky breath.

Where is Silas? What did Lydia mean when she said he would 'pay' for snooping in their flat? What will she do to him?

I still need the milk I came for – it will look odd if I return to the Ricketts' without a full pail – so I go back into the house and head for the kitchen. I let myself in. The room is empty. I can see Annie pottering about outside, but there's no sign of either Lydia or Silas. What's happened? Has Lydia chucked him out of the house? Is he already on his way home?

Something doesn't feel right.

I hesitate, unsure what to do, then walk over to the connecting door between the kitchen and the Community Room. I push it open. Lydia is wiping down the long table that we all sat around at last night's meeting. The table is clear now and back in its usual position in the middle of the room, though the chairs usually tucked underneath are scattered randomly around.

'Hello,' I say.

Lydia looks up. Her cheeks are flushed and strands of hair have escaped from her usually neat ponytail. 'Ah, hello, Asha. What are you doing here?'

I hold out the pail. 'I need to get some milk for the Ricketts'.'

'Of course.' Lydia gives the table another wipe. She's definitely flustered.

I go back to the kitchen and open the fridge, my mind running at one hundred miles an hour. I want to ask Lydia if she knows where Silas is, but if I do, she might suspect I was with him. I reach for the vat of sheep's milk and turn the spigot to fill my pail. Should I confess I was snooping in the study? It feels really unfair that Silas should be the only one to get into trouble. Except . . . he did give himself up for me, and me confessing will make that effort pointless.

I finish filling the pail, call out 'goodbye' and hurry off, taking the path away from the house, round the bend of the island, then climbing up Rickett Hill. The rain is holding off, though dark clouds still loom overhead. From here I can see the paths on either side of the island, all the way back to Silas and Pixie's cottage halfway along on the east side, and my own a little further away on the west.

There's no sign of him. He must have been running at

full pelt to have got home already. Feeling troubled, with the pail full of milk heavy in my hand, I carefully make my way down the hill and along the path to the Ricketts' house. I'm expecting Mum to ask why I've been so long, but she takes the milk from me without a word, then asks me to check on the baby.

As I gaze down at little Nan Rickett in her crib, I remember the photo. I take it out of my pocket and peer properly at the two little girls. The girl on the left with dark, wavy hair is definitely me: I'm smiling at the camera and wearing a smart, shiny pink dress with a lilac lace cardigan. Definitely nothing like the soft, muted natural fabrics Mum has always dressed me in. In fact, now I'm really looking, I'm certain this is the youngest I've ever seen myself. Was it taken before Mum rescued me and brought me to Dimity Island? Mum has always denied having any photos from before our arrival.

I sink down onto the bed next to the crib and peer closely at the other little girl. Her fine white-blonde hair is tied in two blue ribbons, to match the blue of her dress, and her heart-shaped face is turned slightly towards me, her chubby fingers reaching for mine.

It's a beautiful picture, the bond between the two toddlers radiating out of the photo. Something stirs in my soul, my chest tightening.

Who on earth is she?

I turn the picture over. On the back, scrawled in unfamiliar handwriting, it says:

Asha and Willow – 20 months!
Love, J x

Is the *J* on the back for my birth mum, Jasmine? Did she write those words?

I trace them with my finger, then look at the photo again.

'*Willow.*' I say the other little girl's name out loud, hoping it will help me make sense of what I'm seeing. For a split second I feel the pull of a memory – something warm and safe – but it's too fast and too fleeting to make any sense of.

I head back inside. Mum is stirring a big pot of soup on the hob. She looks up as I walk in and smiles. 'I think we've got everything under control,' she says, putting her ladle down.

I walk towards her, holding out the photo. 'Look what I found, Mum! Do you know where it's from?' I ask. 'Or who I'm with in the picture?'

Mum frowns. Takes the photo. She stares at it for a moment.

'Where did you get this?' she asks.

'I . . . I . . .' I think quickly, suddenly conscious that I don't want to get Silas into any further trouble. 'I found it just now when I was getting the milk. It was on the hall floor of the Big House, at the bottom of the stairs.'

Mum looks at me, her frown deepening.

'So how come Lydia and Tem have it?' I demand. 'When was it taken? And who is the other girl? Who is Willow?'

'Honestly, Asha, I've never seen this before,' Mum says shakily, her eyes filling with tears. 'I have no idea who Willow could possibly be.'

I stare at her, taken aback. Mum hardly ever cries, except over wounded animals. I'm suddenly certain that she's hiding something. And, in so doing, is breaking the most fundamental tenet of our island life: the first of the four *T*s – truth.

'You *do* know,' I insist.

'No!' Mum frowns, wiping her eyes. 'You just said you found this photo in Lydia's house. Don't you think that, if I knew about it, I'd have kept it myself?'

This is a good point, but still leaves too many unanswered questions. 'Okay, but who is Willow? Is the *J* on the back for *Jasmine*?'

'I've told you, I don't—'

At that moment, the front door sweeps open and Chola appears — a grubby smear on her cheek and dark shadows of exhaustion under her eyes. Mum shoves the photo in her pocket and fixes a bright smile to her face. 'Hey, Chola! How's the lambing going?'

'Well, thanks. Wow!' Chola exclaims, taking in the gleaming kitchen and the pot of soup on the hob. 'You've worked miracles, Rose.'

Mum blushes. I fidget from foot to foot.

'Mum?' I prod her side. 'Would Chola know about the girl in the photo?'

'What photo?' Chola asks.

'No!' Mum says sharply to me. 'Right, well, Chola, we need to get off. I need to—'

Her words are drowned out as Chola's husband, Winston, and their daughter, Jemma, walk into the house and the room explodes with noisy chatter, everyone talking at once.

'It's always so amazing when you see them for the first time!' Jemma gushes.

'What Tem doesn't know about sheep,' exclaims Winston.

'We're so lucky to have his expertise,' adds Chola.

Mum and I make our excuses and hurry away.

Rain is spitting as we walk along the island path. Mum

is pacing along, head down against the wind. I'm almost having to run to keep up with her.

'Why didn't you want me to ask Chola about the photo?' I demand. 'What aren't you telling me?'

Mum stops dead. She turns to face me. 'I need to speak to Lydia,' she says. 'I want you to go home while I go up to the Big House.'

'But—'

'I'm not going to argue with you,' Mum snaps. 'I need to speak to Lydia. Then we'll talk.'

I fall silent. We're passing the path that leads down to Pixie and Silas's cottage. This is my chance to check in with Silas, make sure he got back okay after Lydia shouted at him.

'Okay,' I say grudgingly. 'But I'm going to see Pixie first.'

'You have chores at home,' Mum says.

What's going on? It's really unlike her to make a fuss about me visiting Pixie.

'Um . . . I want to see if she's got something for me to wear to my party, like you said.'

'Fine, but I don't want you gossiping about that photo.' Mum casts me a quick glance. 'Wait until I've spoken to Lydia – then we'll talk. Okay?'

'Okay,' I say.

Mum speeds away. She's definitely behaving super oddly. I'm certain she knows more than she's saying. But what? I know Lydia brought me and Mum to the island, but it seems really unlikely that Lydia would have a photo of me from before that Mum didn't know about.

As I turn onto the path towards Pixie and Silas's place, the spits of rain become a drizzle. Their cottage is made from the same dark grey granite as ours. A soft plume of smoke curls into the air from the chimney. That must mean Silas is here. Mustn't it?

I give a quick knock, then push the door open and step inside. Pixie is sitting at her mum's sewing machine in the far corner of the room, surrounded by pieces of brightly coloured fabric. She looks up and smiles.

'Hey, Asha, look at these amazing silks I found.'

'They're lovely. Er, where's Silas?'

Pixie shrugs. 'No idea.'

My head spins. Where on earth is he? Across the room, Pixie picks up the pink and orange fabrics and holds them out to me. 'I'm making a jacket with these,' she announces proudly. 'It's going to have actual sleeves. Getting them right is *way* more complicated than anything else I've done.'

'Right,' I say. 'Great, but I *really* need to find Silas. Are you sure you don't know where he is?'

Pixie's face flushes. She puts down the colourful silks.

'I already told you, I don't,' she mumbles. 'Don't you like the sound of the jacket?'

'It's not that,' I say, feeling guilty. I don't want to tell her what Silas was doing earlier, so, ignoring Mum's instructions, I decide to tell her about the photo. 'I just found something . . .' Pixie listens intently as I explain. 'It's just so weird that I haven't seen it before. And the way Mum's acting is even weirder . . .'

'She's probably just worried about upsetting you,' Pixie says. She shuffles in her chair. 'Anyway, whoever this other girl is, it's not like she can have anything to do with you now. I don't really see why it's such a big deal.'

'Well, you aren't adopted with no idea about your past,' I mutter. 'You wouldn't understand.'

The atmosphere tightens. Pixie turns back to the sewing machine, her shoulders stiff with hurt.

'Sorry,' I say quickly. 'That was mean.' I hesitate, hoping Pixie will turn back and accept my apology. Maybe even listen properly to how freaked out I'm feeling. But she doesn't, so I turn and walk outside.

I shut the door behind me and lean against the wall of the porch. Rain is drumming down now on the cottage roof, and the clouds are so low that I can barely make out the top of Rickett Hill. It's damp and chilly. I draw my jacket around my chest and try to collect my thoughts.

Silas's goat, Edison, lifts his head from the weeds he's chomping on as he sniffs my scent.

My mind races, my thoughts ricocheting from the photo to Mum's weird behaviour to Silas and the mystery of his whereabouts. My limbs stiffen with cold as I stand, trying to make sense of everything. I'm roused by the sharp sound of Lydia's voice, like an arrow darting on the wind. I look up. She's coming down the path towards me, speaking very seriously – I can't catch the actual words – with Tem on one side of her, and Mum on the other.

I stand up as they approach.

'Asha!' Lydia nods at me, her waxed jacket crackling as she sweeps past. 'We'll talk in a minute.'

Does she mean about the photo? I look at Mum. 'What's going on?'

'Come on inside, love,' Mum says, her forehead knitted in a frown. 'You're frozen.'

'Yes, let's get inside,' Tem adds, ushering us into the cottage.

Pixie stands up as she sees us, her hand flying to her mouth. 'What is it?' she asks. 'Has something happened to Mum and Dad?'

'No, no, sweetie.' Mum hurries over and puts her arm around Pixie's shoulders.

'It's not your parents.' Lydia's mouth sets in a grim line.

Suddenly, I know what she's going to say next. 'It's Silas.'

'I'm afraid your brother has got himself into trouble,' Tem adds gently, taking off his cap.

My heart skips a beat.

There's a tense silence; then Lydia clears her throat. 'Earlier today I caught Silas in our study. He was vandalizing our files and stealing cash.'

Vandalizing? Stealing? *What is she talking about?*

'Of course we don't have much, but it's very distressing,' Lydia goes on with an injured sniff. She turns to Mum. 'When I caught him, Silas had money in his pocket from the island community savings fund.'

'Oh, goodness!' Mum's face drains of colour.

'No!' I say, unable to listen any longer. 'No *way.*'

Everyone looks at me. Lydia raises her eyebrows. 'Excuse me?'

I meet her hard gaze, my heart pounding. How can I explain that I know she is lying because I was hiding in the room at the time?

'Silas isn't a thief,' I insist.

'I know it's not what we want to believe, but if Lydia says so . . .' Mum gives me a rueful smile.

I glare at her.

'I . . . I don't get it.' Pixie's voice is hollow, her face as white as the sheets I can see through the window, flapping

46

on the line. 'Why would Silas steal?' She leans against Mum, who squeezes her shoulder.

'It's very worrying, I agree,' Tem says. 'We're deeply concerned about him.'

'It's not just the attempted theft,' Lydia adds. 'Silas pushed me and I knocked my head against a shelf. Look.' She lifts her fringe, to show us a dark red bruise on the side of her head.

My jaw drops. Lydia got that bruise because she lunged for Silas and missed, then stumbled and fell against the bookshelf. It had nothing to do with him.

'Oh, *no*.' Pixie's voice trembles. 'Are you sure? I've never seen Silas act like that.'

'I'm afraid so.' Tem shakes his head. 'It's totally unacceptable. I might have been able to live with the theft, but violence is a dealbreaker.'

He's totally bought into Lydia's lies. I glance across at Mum and Pixie. It's obvious from the scared, strained expressions on their faces that they believe her too.

'This is all rubbish!' I snap, my fists balled at my sides. 'There's no way Silas did *any* of those things you're saying.'

Mum and Pixie look horrified. Tem shakes his head sorrowfully.

Lydia raises her eyebrows. 'Are you calling me a liar, Asha?' she asks icily.

I glare at her. Guilt squirms through me. I want to say yes; to explain that I *know* Silas is innocent and that for some reason Lydia is breaking three of the most fundamental rules – truth and trust and transparency – that we live by.

But the very fact that they are so fundamental holds me back. Lydia has too much to lose to let herself be caught out in a lie. Whatever I say, she will find a way to twist it.

I stay silent.

'Of course Asha isn't calling you a liar, Lydia,' Mum insists. 'She's just upset because she's so close to Pixie.' She glances at Pixie, whose face is crumpled, a silent tear leaking down her cheek. 'It's *Pixie* we need to be thinking about right now.'

'That's exactly why we're here,' Tem adds hurriedly. 'For Pixie.'

'Can we call Mum and Dad?' Pixie asks miserably. 'I'm sure they'd come straight home if—'

'We're trying to reach them,' Lydia interrupts. 'The phone coverage where they are is terrible, but we've left messages, and once we hear from them, we'll organize a call.'

'Oh, thank you.' Pixie sniffs.

'In the meantime,' Tem says, 'we don't think you should stay here alone.' He turns to Mum. 'We're hoping,

Rose, that you'll take Pixie with you to your cottage until her parents return. She and Asha are good friends. I'm sure Asha won't mind making room for—'

'What about Silas?' I interrupt, a sense of foreboding sweeping over me.

Tem glances at Lydia. She draws herself up. Her fierce green eyes bore into me. 'We've locked him in the storeroom in the Dimity House cellar.'

It's like a punch to my guts. Lydia is lying about Silas and locking him up just for defying her.

And it's all happened because he was trying to protect me. I shudder, imagining Silas, locked up in the gloomy basement storeroom of Dimity House. Pixie is still weeping. Mum rubs her back.

'It's going to be all right,' she murmurs.

'I'm afraid it had to be done.' Lydia folds her arms.

Tem shakes his head sorrowfully. 'Silas's actions were just so extreme. There have to be consequences.'

'How long will you keep him locked up?' I ask. Surely it won't be for more than a few hours? When Aaron Brickman was a teenager, he broke all the ground-floor windows at Dimity House for a dare, and he just had to write an essay on the four *T*s and do extra farm work to pay for the glass. There's no crime on the island – and very little conflict.

Everyone's always saying what a peaceful, harmonious place it is to live.

'Silas must stay locked up for at least a week,' Lydia says.

'What?' I stare at her, shocked.

Pixie bursts into fresh sobs. Tem looks down at his feet. Lydia gives a sigh of frustration and shifts the bag on her shoulder. As she moves, the photo of me and the other little girl, Willow, pokes out of the bag.

I point to it. Even if I can't help Silas, at least I might be able to get some answers about my past. 'Did you know about that?' I ask. 'Mum said she had to talk to you about it.'

'In a minute, Asha.' Lydia purses her lips, pushing the photo out of sight and zipping the top of her bag. 'Okay,' she says wearily. 'Rose, please help Pixie pack some things.' She indicates her husband. 'Tem will help you carry everything over to your cottage, won't you, Tem?'

'Sure,' Tem says, rubbing his hands awkwardly. 'But please be quick. I need to get back to the lambing.'

Pixie looks up and sniffs. 'What about Edison? Silas wanted me to look after him.'

'We'll take him with us,' Mum says.

Lydia beckons me to the front door. 'Come with me, Asha. We can talk back at the Big House.'

★

I follow Lydia out of the cottage. It's raining hard now, and we make our way along the path in silence. The ground is sodden from all the recent rain and the stone path is slippery – or would be if I wasn't wearing my boots.

Lydia leads me back to Dimity House and, after leaving our coats and boots downstairs, we go up to her and Tem's flat. I've hardly ever been in their apartment, and now here I am on my second visit in just a few hours. The door to Lydia and Tem's bedroom is ajar. I glance inside as we pass. I can just see the edge of the bedside table where the island's emergency mobile phone is charging next to a sturdy brass lamp. Lydia motions me into the living room, which overlooks the beach and jetty – and the roiling grey sea beyond.

We sit down opposite each other. Lydia takes out the photo and lays it on the table in front of me.

'Your mum says you found this at the bottom of the stairs here?' She sounds like this seems very unlikely, and I can feel my cheeks flushing as she glares at me.

'Yes.' I return her gaze, heart pounding at the lie.

'Hmm.' Lydia makes a face. 'Silas says he took it and must have dropped it.' She pauses and my stomach flips over. There goes Silas covering for me again. 'I'm not sure I believe him. He refused to say where he found it originally . . .' She looks at me again.

'What does it mean?' I ask, trying to shift her focus away from the stealing of the photo. 'It was obviously taken from before Mum adopted me . . . but how come *you* had it? Who is the *J* who wrote on the back? Is it my birth mum, Jasmine? And . . . and who is this?' I point to the little blonde girl.

There's a long pause; then Lydia sits back and taps her fingertips together. 'You're old enough to hear the truth, Asha, so I'm going to tell you exactly what happened when your mum found you.'

'I know about that already,' I protest. 'My birth mum died in a car accident on the mainland. Mum – Rose – found me on the rocks by the sea in my baby seat, with the tide coming in . She rescued me – then later she adopted me and brought me here. You helped her.'

'Ye-es,' Lydia says slowly. 'That's all true, except . . .' She hesitates. 'It wasn't a formal adoption.'

'What do you mean?'

Lydia taps her fingers again. 'I mean that we didn't go through the official channels to adopt you. Rose was desperate to keep you, and I was eager to help her, so we bypassed social services.'

'You mean you *kidnapped* me?'

'The word is "abducted" and *no*, that is absolutely *not* what we did.' Lydia waves her hand dismissively. 'We saved you from a childhood spent in a care home, neglected and—'

'Wait . . . Stop!' I leap up. 'Are you saying that you and Mum just *took* me, without even checking if I had a family?'

'Of course I checked,' Lydia says crossly. 'The news reports I saw said that Jasmine was a single mum with no family. That's why I was so sure you'd end up in care. And, believe me, life on the mainland is tough and corrupt enough without wishing the additional demands of the care system on a baby.'

I can't believe it. 'But if the adoption wasn't official, why didn't the police come after me? You're always saying how fierce they are. Didn't they wonder where I was?'

'They assumed that you'd died, like your birth mother,' Lydia explains. 'As you know, her car went over the cliff, then crashed onto the rocks by the sea. Rose found you in your car seat, thrown clear of the car and bawling your head off. After she took you, the car seat was washed out to sea when the tide rose. It was found, with the fastenings broken, on a beach the following day. The news stories I read said that you must have either been killed instantly, like your birth mother, or drowned when your car seat was swept out to sea.'

My head spins. 'But if you found out that from news stories, then you must have found out all sorts of things about my family . . . my real mum and—'

'Rose is your real mum.' Lydia winces. 'Your birth mum sadly passed away when you were a baby. I know nothing about her other than that she was entirely alone in the world. More importantly, Rose loves you like you were her own flesh and blood. You know that, don't you?'

I nod slowly. 'Okay, but she – both of you – still lied about adopting me—'

'We only had your best interests at heart.' Lydia leans forward. 'It's very important you understand this, Asha. In rescuing you, Rose and I were offering you a far better life than the one you would otherwise have had, with no living family to take you in.'

No living family to take me in. I gaze down at the photo again. 'So who is this girl I'm with? How did you get this photo?'

'It was in the bag Rose took when she rescued you,' Lydia says. 'She was in such a panic, she hadn't looked inside it when she came to me. I found the photo in a side pocket.' She pauses. 'I disposed of the bag and everything else – apart from a couple of nappies.'

I frown, the truth is hovering now just outside my

vision, but I still can't quite believe it. 'Why didn't you tell Mum about this picture?' I ask slowly.

'To protect her.' Lydia sighs. 'To spare her from knowing the truth.'

'What truth?' I ask, my throat dry.

'The truth about her.' Lydia points to the little girl sitting beside me in the photo. 'Willow is your twin sister.'

My head spins as the entire world seems to tilt on its axis.

'Willow is my twin sister.' I echo Lydia's words, flatly, trying to take them in. All my life I've wanted siblings, and now, out of the blue, I discover I not only have a sister but a *twin*. I look up at Lydia, meeting her fierce gaze. Angry, hurt words slip out of me: 'You ripped me away from her. You *separated* us. You *left her behind*.'

Lydia shakes her head. 'I didn't do any of those things on purpose,' she insists. 'There was no mention of a sister in the initial news reports I read. It was only later, once we were back on the island, that I realized the Willow in this picture was your twin.' She pauses. 'By then it was too late. We couldn't go back. Remember, Rose and I had bypassed all the official channels. We'd have got into serious trouble if we'd tried to reunite the two of you. And there was no way of bringing Willow here. I had to accept the trade-off: you would lose your sister, but you'd

55

have a wonderful life here on the island with a loving mother instead of going into a care home or risking being fostered by someone much less loving on the mainland, which is, presumably, what happened to poor Willow.' She leans forward, hands clasped in earnestness. 'I still think I made the right choice.'

'It wasn't your choice to make!' I flip the photo over and look at the message on the back again.

Asha and Willow – 20 months!
Love, J x

'So d'you think this *J* is for *Jasmine*?' I demand. 'Like maybe this photo was a copy my mother was going to give someone before she died?'

'I guess so,' Lydia says.

I touch the writing again, feeling the sudden, bitter ache of a connection to the mother who was torn away from me so brutally. This photo represents everything I've lost.

'A real sister,' I murmur. 'A real mum.'

Lydia sighs. 'I appreciate this has all come as a shock, Asha, but as I tried to explain earlier, I think the use of the word "real" in this context is unhelpful and—'

'I don't care what you think.' The words shoot out of

me. Lydia blinks, shocked. I flip the photo right side up again and stare down at the picture of me and Willow. We were clearly, as toddlers, very close. I look up again. 'I want to find my sister,' I say, my determination building as I speak. 'I'm going to the mainland to—'

'Asha, you can't!' Lydia's eyes widen in horror.

'Don't tell me what I can and can't do. I have a *sister*. I want to meet her, to—'

'If you track Willow down, you'll put this entire community in jeopardy.'

'I don't care.'

'No?' Lydia raises an eyebrow. 'Well, maybe you'll care about this: if you find Willow and the truth comes out about how Rose took you, she'll go to jail for child abduction. Possibly for life.'

'But Mum didn't even know about Willow,' I protest.

'That won't make any difference,' Lydia says. 'Rose took you from the scene of the car crash, failed to hand you over to social services and brought you to Dimity Island without the permission of the state.'

'Only because you helped her.' I stare at her. I can just imagine how Lydia would have encouraged and influenced Mum every step of the way. 'There's no way she'd have done anything without you saying it was okay.'

'Don't think you can pin any of this on me, Asha.' Lydia narrows her eyes. 'Make no mistake, if I go down, Rose is going down with me.'

I gasp, shocked by the sudden cruelty in her voice. Before today, I wouldn't have believed Lydia capable of making a threat like this, let alone carrying it out. But now, after everything she's said and done in the past few hours, I don't doubt that she's serious.

Lydia leans forward and picks up the picture of me and Willow. 'Now, I'm going to take this and destroy it. Something I should have done a long time ago.'

'No!' Tears prick at my eyes. 'You can't!'

But before I can stop her, Lydia has reached for a lighter and flicked a flame onto the edge of the photo. The picture flares up, the colourful images destroyed instantly. My stomach drops away. Lydia walks across to the kitchen area and drops it into the big steel sink, watching it burn.

It's gone. Filled with despair, I leap up and race out of the door. Tears blur my vision as I clutch the handrail, stumbling down the stairs to the hall. I glance towards the kitchen door. Silas is down in the cellar. He's the only person I want to speak to right now. I hurry over. The kitchen itself is empty. I'm half expecting the door down to the cellar to be locked, but of course it isn't.

Only the storeroom door is lockable.

I inch my way down the stone steps. The cellar is huge, running the whole length of the house with various storage boxes and bits of farm equipment stacked on either side. The only natural light filters in from the small windows high up on the wall. The storeroom is straight ahead. There's a pad beside it for the electronic key card that opens the door. I tiptoe over and peer in through the reinforced-glass panel in the door. Silas is sitting on a packing crate, his head in his hands. The lamp beside him casts spooky shadows across the shelves stacked with boxes and jars and bottles and dusty sacks.

'Silas!' I hiss.

'Asha?' He hurries over to the door. 'Are you okay? I can't believe what Lydia's done. She's made up this whole story about me hitting her, but I didn't. I—'

'I know,' I say. 'I saw. She stumbled and hurt herself. I wanted to tell everyone, but . . .' I hesitate, feeling ashamed of my cowardice.

'You were right not to say anything.' Silas puts his hand on the glass between us. 'You'd only have given yourself away and then you'd probably be in here with me.' Silas grins – the same smile that a few hours ago would have made my stomach flip over, but now all I can think about is Willow. The twin sister I didn't know I had.

59

'Are you all right, Asha?'

I nod. 'Thank you for covering for me. It's so wrong that Lydia's put you in here.' I grimace. 'I wouldn't be surprised if I end up in here too.'

'Why?' Silas leans closer to the window. 'What's up? Is it something to do with that photo you found? Lydia mentioned it and I said I must have dropped it, but I'm not sure she believed me.'

I swallow hard, pushing down the tears that threaten to rise again.

'I just found out that I have a secret sister,' I say flatly. 'A twin sister called Willow. *That* was the photo: her and me. Lydia lied to Rose about me having a sister, and they abducted me, and now Lydia says Rose will go to jail if I—'

'Wait. *What?* Start from the beginning.'

I quickly explain everything I've just learned about my past.

'That's such an awful thing to do – separate you from your sister.' Silas frowns. 'But . . . hang on. I get why Rose might have thought it was okay to take you if you had no family, especially when she can't have any children herself. But why on earth did Lydia go along with it? *She's* never even wanted kids. Why would she risk going to jail to help Rose keep you?'

60

This particular question hadn't occurred to me. I shake my head. 'All I know is that I have a secret sister and I have to find her.'

We both fall silent.

'I should go,' I say.

'Yes,' he says. 'And, Asha, thank you. For everything.' It sounds like he's saying goodbye.

I narrow my gaze. 'Are you still planning to leave the island?'

Silas nods. 'I'm more determined than ever.'

I take a deep breath. 'Then I'm coming with you. I'm going to get out of here and find Willow, if it's the last thing I do.'

Silas and I talk for a little longer, trying to work out how we can get away from the island. Every option we explore presents massive challenges.

'What about the motorboat?' I suggest. 'I could try looking for the key again.'

Silas shakes his head. 'Lydia isn't stupid. She guessed immediately that's what I was looking for in their apartment. She's already told me she's got Tem constructing a metal cage where the boat is moored. Double the security than before.'

'Oh.' I pause. 'She's told everyone you stole money from them.'

Silas looks away. 'Ah, well, I did do that. I thought I'd need it on the mainland.'

'Oh,' I say, feeling uncomfortable. 'But . . . stealing is wrong.'

'So is locking people up in a cellar and lying about them being violent,' Silas points out. 'Look, I didn't feel great about taking the money either, but I couldn't see how I was going to manage on the mainland without it.'

'How will we manage there now?' I ask.

'I have an uncle not too far from Salthaven. We'll just have to find a way.' Silas hesitates. 'You really don't have to run away with me, Asha. Your mum will be devastated. I feel bad enough about leaving Pixie myself – I don't want her to lose you as well.'

'Mum and Pixie will have each other.' I explain how Pixie has moved in with us.

'Okay, but how will you track Willow down? And – once you have – how will you protect Rose from being arrested?'

'There has to be a way to find Willow,' I insist. 'I have her name. She's got to be registered somewhere. Lydia and Tem are always saying how the state keeps ridiculous amounts of information on people.' I pause. 'I'll find

Willow and make her see that Rose isn't to blame for keeping us apart. If I can do that, I'm sure she'll help protect her by keeping me a secret.'

'I guess that'll work.' Silas doesn't sound very sure.

'It will,' I say. 'Hey, Jacob and Max have a rowing boat. Maybe we could use that?'

Silas gives a mirthless laugh. 'That boat is ancient and leaky. It would barely get us around the island, let alone all the way to the mainland. That's a two-hour journey even with a motor.'

I shrink back, my mind racing. 'I know!' I say, an idea springing into my head. 'We can hide on board the next supply boat. There'll be one on Friday – that's just a few days away.'

Silas nods, slowly. 'That might just work.'

'We should do it once everything's unloaded,' I say excitedly. 'The crew always have a meal in the Community Room at that point, before they head back to the mainland.'

'Yes!' Silas's eyes spark with excitement; then his face falls. 'But what about getting me out of here beforehand?' he asks, pointing to the pad on the door beside him. 'Lydia has a card she uses to open the door. She took it when she left. I know she keeps it on her the whole time. How are we going to get hold of that?'

'I'll find a way,' I say. 'I promise.'

★

Mum and Pixie are working in the garden when I get back home. Pixie is sifting through a tray of what looks like beetroot seedlings, while Mum is digging a small trench a few metres away, near the leek beds. It has been raining and the air feels clearer than before. I've been racking my brains all the way here, about how I'm going to get Silas out of the storeroom on Friday. However, as soon as I see Mum, my thoughts fly back to Willow – and the way I was separated from her.

I know Mum has talked to Lydia but, even if I didn't know, it would be obvious from the anxious way she looks at me as I approach. She leaves Pixie examining the seedlings and hurries over. Without speaking, she takes my hand and leads me inside. We stand opposite each other, in our kitchen. Sunlight streams in through the long window above the countertop and Mum shuffles anxiously from side to side, fiddling with the crescent moon on her necklace. My world shrinks to the pained look in her eyes.

'I didn't know about Willow,' Mum blurts out, wringing her hands. 'Lydia only just told me. I mean, when you showed me the picture I wondered if . . . But . . . I didn't know twelve years ago. I promise.' Tears trickle down her cheeks. 'You have to believe me, Asha, if I'd known you had a twin sister when I found you, I'd *never* have separated you from her.'

'I know, Mum,' I say, my heart softening at the fear and hurt on her face.

'I thought we were *helping* you by taking you, so you wouldn't have to go into the care system on the mainland or risk being taken in by a family that wouldn't really love you.' Mum takes a deep breath.

'I know,' I say again. 'But Lydia should still have told us about Willow.'

I'm expecting Mum to agree instantly, but instead she reaches over to the window ledge and absently rearranges the dried flowers in the nearest pot. She fills the house with nature all year round: sheafs of orange and gold leaves in autumn, holly with bright red berries through the winter and wild flowers in summer.

'I don't think it's fair for you to be cross with Lydia,' she says very carefully.

I'm so astonished that my mouth falls open. 'Seriously?'

'Lydia was just trying to protect me,' Mum continues. 'She knew I'd be devastated to find out you had a sister.'

'But—'

'Just like she knew how lost I was back when I found you. How desperate I was for a baby.'

'Being desperate doesn't justify knowingly taking a child away from its only family.'

'Lydia's explained . . . Jasmine was a single mum and there was no dad or other family in the picture. She didn't know about Willow until . . . until it was too late to turn back without both of us getting into trouble and losing you.' Mum pauses. 'Lydia risked a lot to help me bring you here.'

I shake my head, remembering Silas questioning exactly that. 'Why *did* Lydia take that risk?' I ask. 'What did she get out of it?'

Mum tuts. 'It wasn't transactional like that, Asha. Lydia just wanted to help. I'd already agreed to live on the island and promised the money to her and Tem.'

I frown. 'What money?'

'My inheritance,' Mum explains. 'The money from my parents. I've told you this already – they died the year before I found you. It was one of the reasons I was so confused at the time.'

'I didn't know they left you money.' I sink back against the countertop. It all makes sense now. Lydia needed Mum's money. That's why she helped Mum take me.

'I gave the money to the island because I believed – believe – in what it stands for,' Mum protests. 'You *know* that Lydia does too. She's more committed to the four *T*s than anyone. So don't make out that she manipulated me. She *saved* me.'

There's no arguing with her.

'Whatever, Mum, but this all needs to be put right.' I draw myself up. 'Now I know about Willow, I have to find her.'

Mum stares at me. 'You can't!' she cries. 'If you show yourself on the mainland, Lydia and I will be sent to prison.'

'Not if Willow keeps me a secret,' I point out. 'I'm sure she will if I ask her to.'

'That's very naive of you, Asha,' Mum says, hands on her hips.

'Me, naive? You're the one who thinks Lydia only ever wants to help people when really she just manipulates us into doing what she wants.'

Mum's hand flies to her mouth. For a second I think she's going to argue back, but instead she fingers the point on her crescent moon necklace, then talks as if I hadn't spoken.

'We should get back out to Pixie,' she says, her eyes not meeting mine. 'I don't want to leave her on her own too long – she's so upset about Silas.'

What about me? I'm upset too.

The words stay stuck in my throat, as Mum turns and walks out of the cottage, leaving me alone.

★

The next few days pass slowly. My thoughts skip around, from possible ways I can get the key card for the storeroom off Lydia, to how I'll find Willow once Silas and I get to the mainland. Silas says we can head for his cousins' house; that they'll have phones and computers I can use to track down Willow. Maybe he's right, but it sounds vague. And scary.

Mum throws me nervy glances from time to time – as if I'm a bomb she's worried might explode at any minute – but it's obvious that she's mostly focused on Pixie. Whenever Pixie slouches across the garden or slumps onto the couch, Mum frowns, her concern creating a deep crease in her forehead. I point out that Pixie is only upset because Silas is locked up in the storeroom. Which is entirely down to Lydia.

Of course, Mum immediately leaps to Lydia's defence, just like she did over Lydia lying to her about Willow all those years ago.

'It's very sad about Silas,' Mum mutters, 'but Lydia *had* to do something to discipline him. We have to trust her and Tem to handle this.'

Despite the fact that we're sharing a bedroom, Pixie herself never asks me about Willow – or how I feel about

68

any of the new information I have about my past. I guess she's too caught up in her own problems. Lydia still won't let her visit Silas, insisting that her brother is given time alone to reflect on the seriousness of his actions.

Pixie also tells me that Tem and Lydia are hopeful of getting hold of her parents any day now. 'I know Mum and Dad will come home when they find out what Silas has done and how much trouble he's got himself into,' she says on Wednesday night as we're lying in our beds.

I clench my fists under the bedclothes. Pixie has totally swallowed Lydia's version of what happened.

'Has it occurred to you that maybe Lydia's lying about some of what she said?' I say, staring up at the shadows on the ceiling. 'For one thing, I'm certain Silas didn't hurt her.'

'Then how did she get that bruise on her forehead?' Pixie asks plaintively.

I close my eyes.

'Anyway, Lydia would never lie,' Pixie goes on. 'It's against the four *T*s.'

I itch to tell her the truth, but there's no point. The chances are high that Pixie would just betray me to Lydia and I'd end up locked in the storeroom with Silas, with no chance of helping him escape.

Instead I focus on how I'm going to get us both on the supply boat at the end of the week. I reckon my best chance for getting the key card off Lydia is while the boat is being unloaded. She'll be distracted then – and less likely to notice it's missing.

However I do it, when that boat leaves the island, Silas and I *have* to be on board.

Friday morning, and I wake with a start as Pixie yanks back the curtains and a stream of bright light flashes onto my face. She's already dressed, in a home-made blue tunic with huge white buttons and a pair of white trousers. I peer at the trousers more closely.

'Are those mine?' I ask.

Pixie gives me a sheepish nod. 'I hope you don't mind, but I don't have any white ones, and they go so much better with this top than anything I've got.' She twirls around in the middle of the room and the hem of the tunic flies out around her. 'Do you like it?'

'Yeah, it's great.' I try to fake a bit of enthusiasm, but it's clearly not enough for Pixie. She sticks out her tongue at me, then leaves the room. A moment later I can hear her chatting with Mum, asking for honey on her porridge.

All weekend I've been pushing away the certainty that Mum will be devastated when she finds out I've run away. But then, maybe Pixie is exactly the kind of daughter

Mum wants: someone who does what she's told – and who'll accept whatever version of reality she's offered.

Just like I used to.

I've already been over to Silas's cottage to get him a jumper and rain jacket. I've folded them into the canvas bag that usually contains my school books. I fetch it from under my bed, add a change of clothes for myself and sling it over my shoulder.

'Come on, Asha, you'll be late!' Mum calls.

I cast a final look around my room. What else might I need in the outside world? An excited shiver snakes down my spine at the thought of all the unknown dangers that may be lurking out there. A bit of food for me and Silas? Plus my water bottle? Yes, then – once we're on the mainland – we'll be able to pick berries off bushes and forage for other stuff too.

I hurry out of my room. Mum and Pixie are sitting at the kitchen table tucking into bowls of steaming porridge. A third bowl sits at the empty place next to Pixie. It's decorated with my favourite toppings: pumpkin seeds and the last of the blackberries from the Big House freezer.

'Asha, please come and eat something!' Mum orders.

I shake my head. I'm too excited to feel hungry right now. 'I'll take some rolls with me, have breakfast later.'

A few moments later, with the rolls, some cheese and a full water bottle in my bag, Pixie and I set off. Pixie chatters the whole way to school, mostly about the next thing she's planning to make once her silk jacket is done. She only mentions Silas once.

'I'm going to ask Lydia if she's got hold of Mum and Dad yet. *And* when I can see Silas. He'll be so worried about me.'

I say nothing. All my energy is focused on getting myself and Silas onto the supply boat. And then, once we're on the mainland, finding Willow.

It's one of those March days that can't make up its mind, weather-wise. The wind is fierce, blasting against our faces and sending threatening clouds scudding across the sky. But as Pixie and I round the bend in the island, the sun comes out, glinting off the windows of Dimity House. All the other students – apart from Silas, of course – are in the schoolroom. Jemma Rickett is already hard at work, her head bowed over an A-Level Maths paper. Behind her, Oliver Asiki is whispering loudly to his sister Blossom.

'I still say he shouldn't be locked up.'

'But he *hurt* Lydia, Ol.'

'I don't believe that,' Oliver says, shaking his head.

I glance at Pixie. She shows no sign of having heard them.

As we cross the room, Oliver looks up. Instantly, he's

out of his seat and hurrying over to Pixie. 'Is Silas okay? Have you seen him yet?' he asks.

Pixie shakes her head. 'I'm going to ask Lydia about seeing him now,' she says, shakily.

Oliver and I follow her into the kitchen, where Lydia is bustling along the open cupboards, bending down as she checks what's inside each one. Sally Brickman's daughter-in-law, Eva, is here too, her youngest child strapped on her back as she churns butter from our regular supply of sheep milk.

Oliver and I hang back at the door while Pixie goes over to Lydia. She hesitates for a second, then takes a deep breath.

'Please can I see Silas?' she asks, pressing her hands together like she's praying. 'It's been days.'

Lydia straightens up, unsmiling. She brushes a microscopic piece of fluff from her black shirt. 'I'm afraid not, Pixie,' she says.

I look at Lydia closely. Silas said she keeps the storeroom key card on her person, but I can't see any pockets in her crisply ironed trousers.

'Perhaps giving Silas the time to feel bored will also ensure he reflects on all his actions.' There's something very final about the way Lydia speaks. Pixie stares up at her, clearly intimidated.

I suddenly notice Lydia's familiar waxed jacket hanging

73

over the back of a chair. Could the key card be in one of its pockets? I shuffle sideways towards it, my eyes fixed on Lydia's back.

Don't look round, I plead silently.

'But he's my *brother*,' Pixie says, with more force in her voice than I'd have given her credit for.

'All the more reason to prevent Silas from seeing you. That should encourage him to question whether his recent behaviour is worth all the consequences.'

I reach the jacket and lay my hand on the stiff cloth. I look up. Lydia still has her back to me, while Pixie's eyes are fixed on Lydia. Oliver can't see what I'm doing either – my body is blocking his view. I let my fingers trace down to the jacket's right-side outer pocket, then slide them inside.

Nothing.

'How long are you going to keep Silas locked up?' Pixie sounds really upset.

'It depends,' Lydia snaps. 'Right now, though, it's time for school. The supply boat will be here within the hour, so you need to make the most of your lesson time.'

Pixie doesn't move.

I quickly trace my hand over the rough wax jacket and find the left-hand pocket. My fingers tremble as I slip them inside.

Also empty.

I prod at the cloth, feeling for inside pockets, but there aren't any.

My heart sinks. I take my hand off the jacket and take a step away.

'School, Pixie! All of you!' Lydia's voice rises. *'Now!'*

I reach the door, where Oliver is still standing, as Pixie scuttles towards us. Her eyes brim with tears. I feel suddenly, desperately sorry for her.

'Have a good morning!' Lydia trills.

I glare at her. How dare she bully everyone, then act like it's nothing?

Which is when I notice the strip of thin black plastic peeking out from Lydia's shirt pocket. The worn edge identifies it beyond doubt: there, just above her chest, is the storeroom key card.

How on earth am I going to take it without her noticing?

The morning ticks slowly by. It's odd being here without Silas, but otherwise it's a normal day. The two youngest members of the class – Elisa, the daughter of our teacher Max, and Frank Brickman – are sitting together in the corner, poring over a Geography worksheet. They are both eleven and only moved up to the senior school at the start of the year. Like Jemma, still focused on her

A-Level paper, they are wearing ear defenders to help them concentrate, while Max talks me, Pixie, Oliver and Blossom through our Maths assignment.

Only Blossom is paying proper attention. Pixie looks like she is – she's gazing at Max and nodding – but her eyes are blank and I'm certain she's a million miles away. Oliver is peering down at his text book into which, I happen to know, he's slid an adventure story from the bookshelves behind us. We don't get new books very often and Oliver has read everything at least twice.

I sit quite still, feeling sick to my stomach, while Max burbles on about simultaneous equations. I'm pretending to follow along, but my eyes keep darting to the clock on the wall. The supply boat should be here any moment.

'Let's start with the equation in the first bracket,' Max says. 'If X plus three hundred and fifty-five equals . . .'

I check the clock again, then stare out of the window, watching the glittering tumble of the distant waves.

At last! The supply boat is visible, chugging slowly towards the island across a sparkling sea. In a few minutes it will arrive – and the short window I have for getting the storeroom key card and helping Silas escape will start. My thoughts drift to that black strip of worn plastic poking out of Lydia's shirt pocket—

'And what is four hundred and twenty multiplied by

five, Asha?' Max's voice, suddenly sharp, breaks into my thoughts.

'Er, two thousand, one hundred,' I stammer. Thank goodness I can do mental Maths.

'Mm.' Max frowns at me. 'Very good.'

Flustered, I bend over my textbook for a few minutes. When I next look up, the supply boat is almost at the jetty. The sun glints off its name, *The Cutter*, which is painted in bright white against the black of its hull. Tem is already out there, his orange cap pushed off his face, ready to catch the mooring rope.

A smart rap on the door, and Lydia pokes her head around. 'We'll be ready for the kids in five, please, Max.' She smiles around at us. 'All hands on deck!'

As Lydia vanishes, an air of eager anticipation fills the room. Even Jemma has looked up from her corner and tugged the ear defenders from her head.

Helping unload the boat is something that everyone at school looks forward to. It's a chance to get out of classes and sneak a peek at any interesting new books or games that have arrived with the equipment and grocery orders. If there are any really hefty items Tem and Lydia call for help from the other adults, but usually the supplies are packed in small boxes, easy enough for the senior students – who are right by the jetty, in Dimity House –

to carry. When you're in juniors, the room next door, it's one of the things you most look forward to about moving up to the older class. Sure enough, both Frank and Elisa are already on their feet.

'Finish off your work, please,' Max urges with a sigh, indicating they should sit down again.

Outside, across the beach, one of the crew on the boat throws a rope towards the jetty. Tem catches it and winds it around the nearest cleat. *The Cutter* is our regular supply boat – small, with a single raised cabin at the bow and a stretch of deck behind, all the way down to the seats at the stern. I peer anxiously along its length. Where would be the best place for me and Silas to hide? Under the tarps on the deck? The cabin? Or perhaps in the hold below deck? The boat doesn't usually take long to unload – the two crew members are already off and strolling towards the house where whoever is on kitchen duty will give them a quick meal before their return journey.

Half an hour. That's all the time I have to get Lydia's key, free Silas and find a way onto the boat.

Max releases us from class at last and we hurry to the back door, where Lydia is waiting for us. Her jacket is zipped up, hiding the key card in her shirt pocket from view.

How on earth am I going to get hold of it? She ushers us outside, where the wind whips up and the sun beats down on our faces. We pass the crew on the beach. I recognize them both from previous visits – ruddy-cheeked Kieran and shy, silent Faisal – and say 'hello'.

'Morning!' replies Kieran cheerfully, his voice almost lost in the wind.

Faisal gives a nod.

Lydia has a quick word with them; then they resume their stroll to the house, while the rest of us hurry towards the boat. The wind gets fiercer and the clouds darken as we reach the jetty. I glance back at the house, where the crew are disappearing inside. I imagine Silas shut up in the storeroom and worry again about how on earth I'm going to steal the key card from under Lydia's nose, then get Silas and myself onto the boat without anyone seeing. It seems impossible. I tug my jacket around me, my thoughts shooting to Willow. She's the reason I'm trying to do all of this.

How will she react when I finally track her down? Does she even know I exist?

She might not even want to meet me. But I *have* to find out.

I have to find *her.*

Tem is waiting for us on the boat, checking the cargo on deck against his list.

'Oliver! Jemma!' he orders. 'Please take those bigger boxes between you. Careful. They're not heavy, but they are a bit awkward.'

'I need someone to help me with the boxes below deck,' Lydia says, waving her clipboard.

'I'll do it,' I jump in quickly. Working alongside Lydia will give me the best opportunity to snatch the key card. Though I still have no idea how.

'Good girl!' Lydia nods approvingly, at my enthusiasm. 'Blossom, please come too.'

'Right then.' Tem glances at Pixie and the two younger members of our class. 'You three help Oliver and Jemma. I'll bring the cart round.' He steps back onto the jetty. Jemma immediately takes charge, ordering the younger kids to start on the port side of the boat.

'Come on.' Lydia has already lifted the wooden hatch to the hold, a small, dark space behind the cabin. She props it open and flicks on the switch. Light floods the space below. I've carried boxes up from here on lots of occasions, but this time, as I make my way carefully down the steep steps, I really look around. Is there anything in the hold I can use to help get that key card? Several rows of cardboard boxes line the far wall and a small table and chair are set at the bottom of the steps. Other than that, the hold is empty – literally the only other item is the bare light bulb that dangles from the ceiling at the bottom of the stairs, casting shadows all the way across the room.

Lydia stares disapprovingly at the boxes. 'There's no need for all this wasteful packaging.' She tuts.

'Shall we get started?' Blossom asks.

'Sure.' Lydia says, sounding distracted. 'If we hurry, we should have time to unpack and return all the cardboard to the boat for recycling.'

She settles herself at the little table at the bottom of the stairs, her back to the dangling light bulb, and slaps her clipboard onto the faded table top. 'You girls bring me each box in turn. I'll check them off here – then they can go straight up to the cart.' She bends over the top sheet on her clipboard, frowning slightly as she runs her finger down the list of items.

Blossom and I go back and forth, bringing her a series of small boxes. Once Lydia has checked them off, we carry them upstairs and deposit them on the top deck, where one of the others will take them to the cart that Tem has brought round.

My heart thuds as I trudge up the steps with the next box in my hand. There are lots of things to move, but Blossom and I both work fast. I reckon we'll be done in five minutes or so. As I make the return journey into the stuffy hold, I glance over at Lydia. To my relief, she has removed her jacket and the key card is visible again. How can I take it without her noticing?

The light bulb dangles just above and behind her, lighting her work. One of the reasons for using Blossom and me down here is that we can easily stand underneath the low ceiling. The taller teens, like Oliver and Jemma – not to mention most of the adults – would have to crouch.

The thought gives me an idea. It's risky, but so long as I'm fast, it might just work.

Blossom is on her way out, passing me with two boxes under her arm. I pick up another one and take it up to the top. I glance down. Lydia is still poring over her paperwork, Blossom rummaging for a box at the base of a big stack in the corner. Neither of them are watching me.

Instead of dumping the box on deck, I keep hold of it while I quietly pull the hatch into place behind me. It shuts off the light from outside, but makes little difference to the light in the cabin, which is mostly coming from the bare light bulb. Then I hurry back down, still clutching the box. My heart is in my throat. Blossom has found her next box and is straightening up. Lydia is still bent over her clipboard, the edge of the key card peeking out of her shirt pocket. I move to the side, bend as if I'm picking something up, then turn. It's now or never.

I look up at the light bulb, just a few centimetres above my head, then deliberately ram into it with the box as hard as I can.

A smash of glass. We're plunged into darkness.

'Hey!' Blossom shrieks.

'What the—?' I can hear the scrape of Lydia's chair, the faint shadow of her rising from her seat. I dart forward, until I'm right behind her, then hurl the box down at her feet.

'Argh!' I yelp.

Lydia spins around. 'Asha? What's—?'

'Sorry!' I shriek. 'I bumped into the light!' She's right in front of me now; I can feel the heat of her body. 'Oh, I hate the dark!' I hurl myself into her arms.

'For goodness' sake!' Lydia tries to disentangle herself.

Across the room, Blossom's footsteps sound a hesitant *pad* across the floor. I sense her passing us.

'Asha, let go of me!' Lydia cries.

I can hear Blossom on the steps now. I have seconds until she's at the hatch. I reach the tips of my fingers into Lydia's shirt pocket and slide out the key card.

'The hatch is closed!' Blossom calls, breathlessly. 'It must have slammed shut in the wind.'

I shove the card into my pocket as Blossom pushes the hatch open. A dim glow creeps into the cabin.

'Damn it, we're going to need torches to check everything properly now.' Lydia is already hurrying up the steps.

I check that the whole of the card in my pocket is hidden from view. My fingers close on the worn plastic.

Now to release Silas.

I hurry up the steps after the others, my heart thudding in my chest.

'What on earth happened, Asha?' Lydia is standing on the deck, the wind ruffling her hair. Everyone is staring at me, except Tem and Oliver, who are busy unpacking boxes into the cart. Pixie is on the jetty, standing beside Engels, the gentler of our two horses. She strokes his head, watching me curiously.

'I broke the light.' I look from Blossom to Lydia to Jemma, letting my emotions bubble up into my voice. 'I'm so sorry – I'm terrified of the dark.' As I speak, I force myself not to check my pocket to make sure the key card isn't visible. 'I feel terrible.'

Jemma immediately steps over and puts her arm around me. 'It's okay,' she says. 'No harm done.'

'Indeed.' Lydia tuts impatiently. 'Just an accident.' She looks at Jemma. 'Please take Asha to the Big House, get her a cup of tea, then find a bulb to replace the one that got broken.'

Jemma nods, gently ushering me across the boat and onto the jetty.

Behind us, on the boat, I can hear Lydia issuing instructions to Blossom to take Jemma's place while we wait for the new light bulb.

'And we're going to need a brush and dustpan to sweep up the glass!' Lydia calls out after us.

'On it!' Jemma calls back.

As we walk towards the house, I sniff back my tears. 'Light bulbs are in the cellar,' I say, trying to sound upset and shaky. 'I'll . . . I'll go down and get one for the boat. You get the dustpan and brush from the kitchen. I'm so sorry about all this.'

I let my lips give a little wobble, then worry I've overdone it, but Jemma gives my shoulder another squeeze.

'Don't be so hard on yourself,' she says gently. 'Do you want me to find your mum before I go back to the boat?'

'No.' I gaze at her. 'I just need a bit of time. Maybe I could stay here for a bit?'

Jemma nods. 'Of course. I'm sure Lydia and Tem will understand.'

As we enter Dimity House, she asks, 'Why do you think you got so upset?'

For a second I wonder if she suspects I'm pretending.

'Er, I don't know,' I say, trying to think of a good answer. 'I . . . I think Silas being locked up has really got to me. I didn't think Lydia would go that far.'

'I know,' Jemma says with a rueful smile. 'I was surprised too, but you have to admit, Silas has been pushing things since his parents went away.'

'I guess.' I fall silent as Jemma leads the way into the kitchen. My eyes flicker straight to the door down to the cellar. It stands slightly ajar.

'Hello there.' Samira bustles in from the Community Room, wiping her hands on a tea towel. Over her shoulder, I can see the two crew men from the boat at the long table, now back in its usual position in the middle of the room. Max is chatting with Kieran, the older man, while Faisal – the younger of the two – peers at his phone.

'You all right, girls?' Samira asks. 'Boat unloading done?'

'Not exactly,' Jemma says.

I let her explain what happened on the boat. I may not have seen much of the world, but I know that there are some people who really enjoy a drama, especially the chance to tell everyone about it. And Jemma is definitely one of those people. As she speaks, I murmur that I'm going to get the light bulb and slip down to the cellar. I pick up a bulb from the shelf by the door, then hurry over to the locked storeroom in the corner. I peer through the reinforced-glass. 'Silas?' I hiss.

He's up and over to the door in a second. 'Did you get it?'

'Yes.' I take the key card out of my pocket and slide it across the pad. With a click, the door opens.

Silas is out of the storeroom in a flash. 'Thank you,' he says, brushing his hair out of his eyes.

I nod, thinking how just a few days ago the gesture would have made my stomach give a funny flip. Before I found out about Willow, Silas was like this glamorous rebel, whose desire to escape the island I didn't share or understand. But now that I know about Willow and want to leave too, he seems more like a friend.

'Have they finished unloading the boat?' he whispers.

'Almost,' I say.

'Is the coast clear upstairs?'

'Not yet.'

'Right.' He frowns. 'So . . . so what are we going to—?'

'I have an idea,' I explain. 'When I leave, count to one hundred, then come up. I'll make sure the kitchen is empty.'

'Okay.' Silas nods. 'You've been a good friend, Asha. We're going to get off this island this morning. I *know* it.'

'Can't wait,' I say, smiling. I hold up the key card. 'What shall I do with this?'

'Leave it on the floor by the storeroom door,' Silas says. 'Maybe Lydia will think she dropped it by mistake.'

This doesn't seem very likely, but I'm happy to go with any move that makes it less likely Lydia will realize I stole it from her.

I drop the key card and hurry back upstairs, the light bulb in my hand. Jemma is deep in conversation with Samira, but stops talking when I appear. Clearly she was explaining how I freaked out after the drama on the boat.

I hand her the light bulb. 'Thanks for looking after me, Jemma,' I say, remembering to use the fragile, shaky voice I did earlier.

'No worries.' Jemma glances at Samira. 'I'd better get back, help with the unloading. I think Asha would just like to sit quietly for a bit.'

'Of course,' says Samira. 'I'll make her that cuppa.' She smiles at me.

I force a smile back. I can't let Samira wait for the kettle to boil; Silas will be up here before then. Jemma leaves. I stare after her through the window, watching as she crosses the beach towards the jetty. I need to get Samira out of here. Fast.

'I hear you had quite a fright,' Samira says gently, patting my arm with her soft, fleshy fingers.

I nod, feeling a fresh stab of guilt as I fake a look of

anxiety. 'It was all the broken glass,' I say, letting my voice shake again.

Samira sighs. 'A nice cup of chamomile will see you right.'

I glance across to the door that leads to the cellar. I'm certain Silas's count to one hundred must be finished by now. I turn back to Samira.

'Would you mind if *I* made it?' I say softly. 'You could go and chat to Max and the others next door? I just need a moment by myself.'

'Of course,' Samira says, with another pat. 'If you're sure, Asha?'

I nod again. Samira leaves the kitchen through the door to the Community Room. She pulls it half shut and disappears from view.

I hurry over to the cellar steps. Silas is just appearing, tiptoeing up the stairs. I put my finger to my lips, then glance towards the Community Room door. The faint sound of voices drifts towards us.

Silas emerges, silently, into the kitchen. Keeping close to the wall, he hurries towards the door that leads out to the hall. He turns and looks expectantly at me. I scuttle over to join him and we creep across the hall, into the empty senior schoolroom. I make straight for my desk and pick up the bag I left underneath it. Silas stops in his tracks.

'I should leave Pixie a message,' he says, suddenly sounding uncertain.

I sling the bag across my body and point through the window. Tem and Oliver are already leading Engels away from *The Cutter* along the jetty. The cart trundles behind them, while everyone else walks beside it.

'There isn't time,' I say.

'I have to.' Silas grabs a pad from the stack by the teacher's desk and scribbles a note. He tears off the sheet and puts it on the desk, under the globe.

'There,' he says. 'I just told her to look after Edison and not to worry about me. That I'll be in touch as soon as I can.'

Outside, Engels is plodding across the beach, one carefully placed hoof after another, pulling the cart. Tem, Lydia and Jemma are still strolling beside him, but the others have all run on ahead and are almost at the house.

'Come on!' I hurry to the back door and slip outside, Silas right behind me. The wind is still gusting hard and I brush my hair off my face, frowning with concentration. We reach the edge of the wall and peer round. The cart is off the beach now and on the sloping path that leads up to the house.

'Another few seconds,' I breathe. 'Once they're unloading, they're less likely to see us.'

'We can't wait,' Silas hisses. 'We have to go before the crew come out.'

He's right, though it's a risk. 'Okay,' I whisper. 'Let's go!'

Together we speed off across the raised wooden deck that partially surrounds Dimity House. I try to run as lightly as possible, resisting the temptation to look over my shoulder and see if we've been spotted.

Down the rickety wooden steps, we dive into the bushes that form a natural barrier between the house and the beach. I squat down, my hands on the damp earth. It's calming. I peer through the leaves, the cold air whipping across my face.

No one has noticed us.

I turn, looking across the beach to the jetty. It's not far, but our only route there is totally exposed. Anyone looking out of the window is bound to spot us.

'Keep low,' Silas orders. He sets off at a run.

I look back at the house one last time. Beyond it, Mum is working away in our garden, completely unaware I'm about to run away. It suddenly strikes me just how devastated she will be that I've gone. But what else can I do? I can't waste another minute. Mum might not want me to go to Willow, but she's my twin sister. I need to meet her. I have the *right* to meet her. I set off after Silas, crouching as I run. He stops just before the jetty, ducking behind the large rock to the right. I run up and fling myself down beside him.

'Just the jetty to go,' he says, eyes sparkling. 'Then we can get on board and—'

'Asha!' *'Asha!'* Tem and Jemma call.

'Where are you, Asha?' Pixie shouts.

'Oh, no,' I gasp.

Silas and I exchange a worried look. I peer over the rock. Tem, Jemma and Pixie are on the deck outside Dimity House, looking across the beach in our direction. Tem cups his hands and calls my name again.

'She was *very* upset.' Jemma's voice carries clearly on the wind.

'We need to find her,' Tem says sounding concerned. 'Make sure she's all right.'

Even in the panic of the moment, it strikes me how ironic it is that everyone is so much more worried about my reaction to a broken light bulb than to a long lost sister.

'This isn't good,' Silas mutters. 'If we move now, they're bound to see us.'

I stare at him. After all this effort, are we really going to be stopped at this final moment?

I take off my bag and shove it at Silas. 'Go without me. Get on the boat.'

'But—'

'It's *me* they're looking for. They haven't even realized you're missing yet. I'll go back. Distract them. Just promise me you'll try and find Willow when you get to the mainland. Willow Hope. Same date of birth as me — twenty-second of March.'

'But where does she live?' Silas asks.

'I don't know, but our mum died in Bridmouth, so—'

'Asha!' That's Pixie again. She sounds close, like she's on the beach just metres away.

'Are you sure about this?' Silas grips my arm.

For an answer, I lean forward and give him a swift, fierce hug.

'If I find a way to reach Willow, I'll let you know,' Silas whispers in my ear. 'I promise.'

I tear myself away from him and stand up. Pixie is just across the beach.

I race over to meet her.

'Are you okay?' she asks. 'Everyone's been freaking out cos you were so upset earlier.'

'I'm fine.' I walk past her, forcing her to turn so we're both facing the house, our backs to the spot on the beach where Silas is hiding. I have to stop anyone seeing him. Up at the house, Tem waves his cap at me.

'Come on!' I urge Pixie, then run towards him.

As I race up the steps to the deck, Jemma and Tem

hurry over. I can see Kieran and Faisal tugging on their boots just inside the house. Another minute, and they'll be out here, striding back to *The Cutter*.

I talk fast and loud, trying to keep everyone's attention on me so that Silas has time to get to the boat. 'I'm so sorry to worry everyone – I just needed some air . . .' I gabble. 'I gave myself a fright, but I'm fine now.'

'You just had a shock,' Tem says, patting my arm. 'You'll be right as rain in a minute.'

I nod as Kieran and Faisal open the back door and come out to join us. Everyone says goodbye; then the two men head across the beach. I let myself turn now, my stomach twisting with worry that Silas might still be in view. But there's no sign of him. He must already be hiding on the boat. We all watch as the two crew men stride along the jetty, unhitch the mooring rope and jump on board. The engine revs. Kieran waves. Everyone waves back. I hold my breath. Surely Silas is free now?

'Where is he?' Lydia storms out of Dimity House. She's holding Silas's note for Pixie in one hand and the storeroom key card in the other.

'What?' Tem's head jerks up. 'Who?'

'Silas,' Lydia snarls. 'He's gone. Someone must have let him out. I found this on the cellar floor.' She holds out the key card. 'Goodness knows how it got there. I'm sure I didn't drop it earlier.'

I look, resolutely, out across the sea. The boat starts to chug away as Lydia pushes past me, her hands to her head.

'There!' She points at the boat. 'Silas must be—' Her remaining words are lost as she flies off, tearing across the beach.

Tem sets off after her. We watch as they race along the jetty, waving their arms at the boat. But it's picking up speed now and a second later moves westwards, around the bend in the island and out of sight.

I spend the rest of the day worrying that Lydia will work out it was me who helped Silas. As he said, she's not stupid. Sure enough, she turns up at our cottage just before sunset, while Mum and I are preparing a vegetable curry for supper. Pixie, who hasn't stopped crying all day as she reads and rereads Silas's note, is outside checking on Edison and feeding the hens. As we chop cauliflower and potatoes, Mum asks quietly if I had any idea Silas was planning on running off earlier.

I shrug and she frowns. Then a sharp rap on the door saves me from her next question. Lydia swoops in, a severe look in her eyes. She stands in our living room, radiating anger.

'Hello,' Mum says, uncertainly. Her fingers reach for the little crescent moon around her neck. 'Is something the matter?'

Lydia raises her hand slowly and points at me. Her forehead creases in a deep frown. 'It took me a while to work it out, but *you* took my key card, Asha, didn't you? You broke the light on the boat deliberately, then stole the key card and went back to the house – all so you could help Silas escape.'

I jut out my chin. A self-preservatory instinct tells me to deny everything, but the truth is I'm proud of what I did to help Silas.

'Asha?' Mum's hand is over her mouth. 'What is—?' She turns to Lydia. 'I'm sorry, but you have to be wrong about this,' she says. 'Asha would never—'

'Yes,' I interrupt. 'I helped him.'

Mum gasps.

Lydia purses her lips. 'What on earth did he say to persuade you to do that?'

I frown. She's making it sound like Silas manipulated me. I'm itching to tell her I was planning to leave too, to look for Willow in spite of her insistence that I shouldn't. But I stop myself. 'Silas didn't have to say anything,' I protest. 'You locked him up – and you lied about him hurting you. You just wanted him out of the way and—'

'Asha!' Mum's shocked voice stops me in my tracks.

'You're *still* accusing me of lying?' Lydia demands. 'On the say-so of a violent troublemaker?'

I hesitate. I want, badly, to explain I was there, in her study at the time, but it won't make any difference to Silas now. I look down at my feet and say nothing.

'Do you realize what you've done?' Lydia goes on. 'You've put Silas in terrible danger, alone on the mainland.'

My head snaps up. 'Silas can look after himself,' I insist.

'And what about Pixie?' Lydia says, her voice like ice. 'I don't suppose either of you thought about the effect his departure might have on her? It was already tough, spending all this time without her parents. And now she doesn't even have her brother.' Lydia pauses and gives a haughty sniff. 'That isn't how friends act, is it?'

'You're twisting things,' I say, my fury rising. 'Silas and I *did* think about Pixie. And she was *already* without Silas because you locked him up and wouldn't let her see him.'

Lydia gasps, clearly shocked at my standing up to her. She glares at me and, though it's hard to hold my ground, I glare back.

'Anyway,' I go on, 'Pixie's parents will be home soon, won't they?'

'I'm so sorry, Lydia,' Mum says, fingers fluttering anxiously. 'I don't know what's got into her.'

'Mmm.' Lydia sniffs again. 'Clearly Silas was more of a malign influence than we realized.' She pauses. 'Your actions will have to be punished, Asha.'

'That's not fair!' I protest.

'Please, Lydia, I'm sure she's sorry—' Mum starts.

Lydia holds up her hand to stop us both. 'I'm not proposing to lock Asha up like I did Silas, just that she should do some extra cleaning in the Dimity House kitchen and write an essay on the consequences of her actions.'

'What consequences?' I can't resist saying. 'The main one I can see is that Silas has managed to get away from you.'

Mum's eyes widen with shock. 'Asha, why are you behaving like this?'

'An essay on the four *T*s, and why they're important,' Lydia snaps. 'On how truth, tolerance, transparency and trust are behind the rules on the island, and why these matter. And the consequences when they're broken – such as the dangerous situation you've helped Silas put himself in.'

I open my mouth to say that it's ironic Lydia wants me to write about how important the four *T*s are, when she's totally ignored those same principles herself.

'You *helped* him, Asha?' Pixie's voice cracks as she speaks.

We all spin round. She's standing at the back door, her eyes fixed on me.

'You *helped* Silas leave? And you didn't say anything to me?'

'I'm . . . I'm sorry, Pixie, but there wasn't a choice,' I stammer. 'I didn't mean to hurt you.'

Mum draws her into a hug as Lydia flings a final, contemptuous look in my direction.

'Your punishment begins tomorrow!' she says, then stalks to the door and storms out.

'Please, Pixie,' I plead. 'Silas *had* to leave. Neither of us—'

'I'll never forgive you!' Pixie lifts her head from Mum's shoulder, eyes glinting with fury as she sobs. '*Never.*'

I stare at her, a heavy feeling settling in my belly. Silas has done it. He's got away.

But I am still here. No closer to finding Willow than I was before.

WILLOW

Traffic roars along the main road, but I barely hear it. I stand on the dusty side street, outside my back garden, and stare at the boy who has just told me that my dead twin sister is still alive. Tears prick at my eyes. Who is he? And why he has come to my house to tell me such a cruel lie? Has somebody I know sent him? Who would want to wind me up that badly?

'Willow, please, I didn't mean to upset you. I realize it's a shock to—'

'To hear that my sister is alive?' I glare at him. 'I'd say that's a bit more than a shock.'

'I know – I'm sorry!' The boy darts over. 'I . . . Listen . . . My name is Silas and I'm Asha's friend. A week ago, she helped me es—'

'Asha's dead!' The words fire out of me like bullets from a gun. 'She was in a car crash when we were babies. Her body was washed out to sea.'

The boy, Silas, recoils. 'No,' he says, frowning. 'No. Rose rescued her from the accident. She saved Asha's life. Her mum, Rose, she—'

'Our mum *died*.' My voice rises. 'And she wasn't called Rose.'

'I know. Your birth mother was called Jasmine — Jasmine Hope.'

I stare at him, shocked that he knows this. For the first time, doubt enters my mind. What Silas is telling me is mad, but he doesn't seem crazy in the slightest. Nor is he acting like someone who's been sent to wind me up.

'How did you know where I live?' I ask.

'Asha knew her birth mum died near Bridmouth, so I called round all the schools in the area and gave your name and year.'

'Seriously?'

He nods. 'I kept saying I had a message for you about a doctor's appointment and eventually I called your school, which I knew because the receptionist said she'd pass on the message. Then I pretended I'd made a mistake and hung up, got on a bus — several buses, actually — and travelled across the country to your school.'

'You came to my school?' I frown. 'Were you there earlier?'

Silas nods. 'I waited outside and kept asking people where you were and eventually someone pointed you out. I meant to come straight over and talk to you, but . . .' He looks down. 'I lost my nerve, so I followed you back here.'

A shiver snakes down my back. No wonder I felt like I was being watched earlier.

'But why?' I ask. 'Why go to all that trouble?'

'Because Asha wants nothing more than to find you. She was supposed to come with me, but . . . but it didn't work out, so I promised her I'd find you myself and help the two of you make contact.'

I stare at him, a million questions bubbling in my head. 'So where is she? Where is Asha?'

Silas shifts uncomfortably. 'I can't tell you until you promise you won't go to the police.'

'The police?' All my earlier suspicions rise up again. Surely there's no legitimate version of Silas's story that wouldn't involve me going straight to the authorities? 'What are you talking about?'

'Asha doesn't want her mum – Rose – getting into trouble.'

I frown. 'Rose . . . as in the woman who rescued her from the accident?' My eyes widen. 'Did Rose abduct her?'

'It wasn't like that.' Silas pauses. 'You see, Rose genuinely believed she was saving Asha from a terrible life.'

'How could she think that?' I shake my head. '*Why* would she?'

'It's hard to explain, but what matters is that Rose had

no idea you existed. She would never have deliberately kept Asha away from you—' A car drives past, belching exhaust into the road. Silas takes a step closer to me, the sun glinting off the metal buttons on his jacket. 'You need to promise you'll keep Asha a secret – not just from the police but from anyone else who might tell them.'

How naive does he think I am? Older teenage boys appearing out of the blue and telling you to keep a secret from your family is basically Stranger Danger Alert 101.

'I don't believe any of this,' I say, keeping my voice calm and steady. I put my hand on the gate in the fence. 'I'm going inside now.'

'Wait!' The boy holds out his hands. 'I need to give Asha a way to contact you directly.'

'No.' I open the gate, edging closer to the safety of my back garden. I just want to get away from him.

'But I have to get back home.' He frowns. 'Couldn't you at least give me your mobile number? '

'I already told you: no!'

'What about your social media? Which ones are you on? Instagram? TikTok? NatterSnap?'

I blink, rapidly, fear rising inside me. 'Go away!' I shout.

Then I hurry back into the garden and slam and bolt the gate. I race back into the house, my heart pounding.

Dad is still sitting at the kitchen table, but there's no

sign of either the boys or Becky. The spilt sugar is swept up and the shopping put away. A mug of tea has been poured and left for me in my favourite Hello Kitty mug.

Dad looks up. Sees my distraught expression.

'What's the matter?' He stands up and walks over.

I can hardly bring myself to speak.

'Willow?' Dad touches my arm. 'Whoa, you're freezing. What on earth has—?'

'A boy just came round . . . I saw him just outside the back garden. He . . . says that Asha is alive.' The words tumble out of me.

Dad's jaw drops. 'A boy says that Asha . . . ?' He trails off. 'What boy?'

'I don't know. He said his name was Silas.'

'Is he still there?' Dad is already out of the door before I can answer. I follow him across the garden to the gate, which he unbolts and flings open.

We go out to the street, but there's no sign of Silas.

'Does this boy go to your school?' Dad asks, as we head back inside.

'No, er, I don't think so.' I walk into the warmth of the kitchen, tears pricking at my eyes. 'He said that he'd escaped from somewhere and that Asha had been supposed to come too but she hadn't made it and he wanted to help me contact her but . . . but I wasn't allowed to tell anyone, like you or the police or . . .' I dissolve into sobs.

'Hey, sweetheart, come here.' Dad pulls me into a hug and I inhale the familiar herby scent of his aftershave through his rough wool jumper. 'It sounds like a horrible wind-up to me.'

'I know – it did to me too.' I draw away. 'But suppose it's true? Suppose Asha is alive?'

Dad shakes his head. 'Come on, that doesn't make any sense,' he says. 'From the sounds of it, Silas's story is all over the place.' He frowns. 'Tell me exactly what he said.'

I go over the conversation again. Becky comes in halfway through, so I repeat bits of it for her.

'It's so weird,' she muses. 'Why would a random stranger come up with such a crazy story?'

I shrug. Dad shudders. I get the sense he's more upset about Silas saying Asha is alive than he's letting on.

'Just try and put it out of your mind, Willow,' he says firmly. 'But definitely let me know if that boy approaches you again and we'll call the police.'

'Absolutely,' Becky agrees. 'In the meantime, there's your birthday to look forward to.' I smile at this very obvious effort to change the subject. 'We'll have a special dinner on the day itself, then do the big family lunch next weekend.'

'Are my cousins coming, then?' I ask.

'Yes,' says Dad. 'I called your Uncle Jam just now.' He hesitates. 'Now promise me you'll put this boy out of your head.'

ASHA

It's nearly two weeks since Silas left the island, and the weather, after starting to get all sunny and spring-like, reverts to almost constant rain for my birthday.

Mum bakes me a chocolate cake, which she knows is my favourite. Meanwhile, Pixie manages to set aside her anger over what she sees as my betrayal in helping Silas escape and gives me a beautiful green dress as a birthday present.

'I made it from an old skirt of Sally Brickman's,' she tells me proudly. 'It's the best design I've ever done.'

'It's amazing,' I say, trying in on. It fits perfectly. I smile at Pixie. I know this is a peace offering from her and feel both grateful and relieved that our friendship is still intact after her outburst two weeks ago. I step over and give her a big hug. 'Thank you so much. It will be perfect this Saturday, for the spring equinox party.'

Pixie grins and Mum claps her hands together, clearly delighted that I'm showing an interest in the party, rather than complaining about Lydia and the 'punishment' essay she made me write yet again.

Little does she know that, underneath, my real mood matches the damp gloom outside. I am stuck here, on Dimity Island, while Willow is out there on the mainland, having her own birthday and, probably, not even aware I exist. I've thought about it a lot and it seems obvious that if the police and the news reports at the time assumed I was dead, as Lydia says, then Willow must think that too.

I can't bear it. Just as I can't bear being here with Lydia bossing everyone around and ranting on about the importance of the four *T*s when she's betrayed every single one of them.

But what can I do? I'm desperate to leave the island and find Willow, but I have no way of contacting her – and no idea how to get to her even if I did. Without Silas, it all seems impossible.

The first supply boat since Silas's escape arrives on Friday, two days after my birthday. Lydia and Tem have already interrogated Kieran, the co-owner, over the phone, demanding to know if he knew he had a stowaway on board. Kieran says he and Faisal had no idea, claiming that Silas must have hidden below deck and snuck out when they weren't looking, back in Salthaven. I'm not sure if Lydia believes him. Either way, she has new rules in place, which means that instead of the crew being invited into Dimity House for their lunch, Tem takes it out to them and eats with them on board.

After school, I throw myself into my chores, clearing out the hen house and laying down fresh straw. I'm alone. Tomorrow is the spring equinox party and Mum is staying late at the Big House to do some extra baking, while Lydia called Pixie away at the end of our last class.

The light is just fading from another gloomy day, when Pixie finally appears. There's an anxious look on her face as she walks over. It's not that cold, but there's something unsettling about her expression and I shiver, tugging my jacket around me.

'Lydia finally got a message from Mum and Dad,' she says. 'They're trying to get home as fast as possible though it'll still probably take a couple of weeks – they have to arrange transport. I can't wait to see them.'

I gaze at her, wondering why she doesn't look happier. 'That's good, isn't it?' I ask.

'And I got a letter from Silas,' Pixie says.

My eyes widen.

'It came on the supply boat this morning. Lydia opened it – she recognized Silas's handwriting.'

'That's outrageous – she shouldn't have—'

'She says she has the right, as Mum and Dad are away.'

'That figures,' I mutter. 'What does Silas say? Is he okay?'

'He's fine.' Pixie's face relaxes with relief. 'He says he's safe and staying with one of our uncles. I didn't even remember we had that uncle, but Silas looked him up and he's letting Silas stay until Mum and Dad get home.'

'Really?'

'Yeah, it also looks like Mum and Dad have agreed to discuss Silas moving to the mainland and starting early at sixth form. I still don't understand why he's so desperate to leave the island, but at least he's safe.'

'Wow.' I'm pleased for Silas, of course, but it's still a blow to hear that he probably won't be back here any time soon.

'Anyway,' Pixie goes on, 'Silas says he's on some social media app called NatterSnap. There's instructions in the letter for using it, but I've got no idea.' She pauses. 'I think Lydia wanted to delete that bit – she's crossed out his username so I can't see it – but I guess she thought she shouldn't mess with the letter too much, in case Mum and Dad minded.'

'Right.'

Pixie rummages in her bag. 'Anyway, the reason I'm telling you is because Silas specifically asked me to show it you – his letter, I mean. Lydia made me promise I wouldn't, but, well . . .' She pulls out a folded sheet of paper.

My jaw drops. 'Really?'

Pixie nods. 'He says you're a good friend, which I guess you are.' She looks awkwardly at me, a tiny smile curling around her lips, then hands me the paper.

Heart beating fast, I unfold the letter, scanning down past Silas's reassurances that he's safe and his instructions on how to access NatterSnap, the social media app Pixie mentioned. I get to the final paragraph. It starts with Silas's username, unreadable now Lydia has crossed it out:

@~~_____~~ is my handle on the NatterSnap app. Please use it if you can. when I left the island the hardest thing was knowing that you'd be upset but I had to go, you have to understand that, Pixie. Please, please know that leaving was only possible because I was sure Rose would be there to look after you, make sure you're okay. And Asha, she's a good friend and the only person on the island I really trust, so you should too. She was there 4 me whenever I needed. I'm sorry I missed her birthday, it was on 22 March I think. Please show her this message. Remember, I'm ON NATTERSNAP, you can reach me whenever you want.

He signs off with his name, a row of xxx and a string of numbers underneath.

I stare perplexed at the last few lines. Why does Silas

write: *Please show her this message*? There *isn't* a message. Unless he means the whole letter, like Pixie obviously thought.

I read the last paragraph again. Maybe there *is* a message here . . . something Silas has hidden so that only I'll spot it. Except he hasn't hidden anything: there's no code, no—

I gasp as I suddenly see it. Silas *has* hidden a message. And it's in plain sight. The letters that start each line, when you put them together, spell out:

@willow22

And then, at the start of the next line, in capitals . . . ON NATTERSNAP.

That's his message: that I can reach Willow on this social media app, which he's explained how to access at the start of the letter! I glance up at Pixie, excitement fizzing inside me.

'What?' she asks.

I'm desperate to tell her what I've just worked out, but I don't dare. I can't be sure she won't blab about my discovery to Mum – or Lydia.

'Nothing,' I say. 'We should go inside. Mum will want help with the dinner.'

112

I hand the letter back to Pixie and follow her indoors. I can't stop myself from smiling. Not only has Silas been thinking of me, but he's found Willow for me as well — and shown me the first step I need to reach her.

Now all I need is a way to make contact.

WILLOW

The Friday after my birthday, I have a fun evening with some friends from school. We try on wigs and make videos and eat pizza. Someone even produces some cupcakes with candles in, which is really sweet of them. It's nice to hang out with my mates for a few hours, but I think about Asha the whole time, as I have done all week since Silas's visit.

I'm close to lots of people, but I've never had a particular best friend. Is a bestie what having a twin sister would feel like?

I don't tell my friends about Silas's visit – or how he told me Asha is still alive. It's not just that it feels too raw and upsetting to talk about. It's that I don't think any of my friends, with their normal families and NatterSnap obsessions, would understand.

Dad picks me up – and doesn't stop talking about tomorrow's family lunch party all the way home. Apparently Becky has made two different lasagnes and a trifle. 'Uncle Jam's coming with Lauren and Ellen, and so are Auntie Jade and your cousin Harlan. Plus a few others I don't know so well.'

Back home, Becky shoos me up to bed. I get into my pyjamas and post some of tonight's videos on NatterSnap. There's an alert on my DMs. I flick the new message open without thinking. It's from @freedomvictory and reads:

Hey, Willow, it's me, Silas, the boy from last weekend in the blue hoodie. I know you didn't believe me, but I was telling the truth about Asha. She should be in touch soon herself. Good luck!

I drop the phone on my duvet like it's scalding hot. All the fuzzy joy from the evening with my friends evaporates. Is this guy stalking me? How dare he just slide into my DMs?

I snatch the phone back up and write:

How did you find me?

I wait, my heart pounding. A reply arrives after a few minutes.

I just searched for people on socials with your name, then checked out their photos. I promise I'm not trying to hurt

115

or frighten you. But Asha is my friend and I want to help the two of you find each other.

I hesitate, my finger poised over the screen. I have the same, weird sensation I did when I met Silas in person. Like everything he says makes sense but is also totally crazy. Part of me wants to close down the conversation, but instead I reply again:

If you really want to help, tell me where Asha is.

A longer pause; then Silas replies:

I'll tell you, but only if you promise not to go to the police.

My heart sinks. Can't he see how suspicious that looks?

My mind now made up, I block Silas from sending any more DMs. Should I tell Dad that he messaged me? I'm still thinking about that, when I fall asleep.

ASHA

It's past midnight and time to put my plan into action. Across the room from me on her pull-out bed, Pixie's slow, even breathing tells me she is fast asleep. I sit up, my heart thudding, and quietly put on the joggers, sweatshirt and trainers I left beside the bed. The air is chilly as I creep out of the bedroom. As I pass Mum's room, she mutters something in her sleep. I freeze and glance around. But she is quiet again, settling immediately into a light, snuffly snore. Moonlight streams in through the living-room window. I take my jacket and scarf from the peg at the front door, then ease the handle round. I hold my breath as I pull the door gently open, slip out and shut it softly behind me. A cold breeze whips at my face as I pick my way down to the path. The solar lamps have almost lost their power, casting only a muffled glow across the track and sending shadows scooting over the grass on either side. I wrap my scarf around my neck and zip up my jacket, then race to Dimity House.

The building is in darkness. There's something spooky about the way it forms a gloomy black outline against the moonlit glow of the sea beyond. A shiver runs down my spine as I ease the front door open and creep inside.

My footsteps whisper a faint echo as I pad across the hall, then make my way up the stairs. I hesitate by the bedroom door. It's ajar, the room beyond completely silent. I creep inside, every muscle tense. I've never come all the way into Tem and Lydia's bedroom before and not only is it bigger than mine or Mum's – it's also way fancier. Instead of a narrow, roughly hewn wooden base and faded duvet, the bed is broad, with a gleaming brass bedhead and a silky coverlet.

Silas's accusation from all those weeks ago echoes in my head: *Why should Tem and Lydia have such nice stuff when the rest of us don't?*

The two of them are lying asleep, their faces lit by the sliver of moonlight filtering in from the crack in the curtains. Lydia's right hand is just visible, her fingers peeking out from under the quilt. The metal case of her phone glints on the bedside table. It's plugged in – charging – just like it was when I talked to Lydia up here nearly three weeks ago.

Holding my breath, I tiptoe over and ease the phone out of its charger. My heart thumps as I remember Silas explaining that Lydia's phone only opens to her fingerprint.

I press my own fingertip on the button at the base of the mobile, willing it to recognize me.

Of course it doesn't.

I crouch down. I take Lydia's forefinger gently between my own finger and thumb, then press it against the button at the base. Blue light fills the room. I stifle a gasp. Lydia screws up her eyes, drawing back her hand. Across the bed, Tem grunts in his sleep. I dart back, gripping the phone. My heart thuds as I look down at the screen. Yes! It's open.

I tear down the stairs, jumping lightly over the creaky step, then fly into the senior schoolroom. I ease the door shut behind me. The screen is full of tiny icons. My hands shake as I swipe to the next page. And the next. It's all icons: incomprehensible to me. Panic whirls in my head. I blow out my breath, trying to calm my furious heartbeat.

What did Silas say in his letter to Pixie?

Look for the App Store, then download NatterSnap.

The App Store icon is on the third page. I open it, then find the little search bar and type in the word 'NatterSnap'.

The NatterSnap icon appears, in blue and pink, just as Silas described. My throat is dry as I follow his instructions for getting the app. I sign up and log in, using my first name along with my birth mum's surname: *Hope.* Surely that will help Willow recognize me.

A tiny wheel appears on the screen, whirling round and round. I wait, staring at it. Is this normal? Silas didn't say anything about—

The wheel stops and the app opens.

Now for the really complicated bit. I find the little search bar again and type in 'Willow22'.

A photo of a girl's face appears on the screen. Is that her? I peer anxiously at the picture. She looks a lot older than I am, with high cheekbones and shining waves of blonde hair cascading over her shoulders. Her skin is smooth and fair and her lips a perfect bow shape. She has a dainty nose and thick, dark lashes. She looks like the models Lydia showed us in the 'Oppression through Images' talk she gave us last year.

Nothing like me.

I wasn't expecting us to look alike, of course – the photo I found of us as babies made it clear we had different colouring – but I also wasn't expecting Willow to be so beautiful. So glamorous. So grown-up-looking.

A noise sounds above – the creak of a door, then a shuffling sound as if someone is crossing the landing.

Is that Lydia? Will she notice her phone is gone?

I make a quick decision: no way am I going to risk replacing the mobile upstairs where I found it. No, I'll leave it in the hall and hope that Lydia just thinks she left it there by accident.

The shuffling stops. Silence fills the house again.

My heart hammers against my ribs as I try to focus on Silas's final instruction.

To call, press the square with the arrow beside her picture.

I find the square and tap it lightly. The screen shifts to a dark background, then asks me if I want to make a video call. That means I'll be able to see the face of the person receiving the call. I press the little lozenge and the phone rings, a soft, low chiming sound. Once. Twice. A third time. A fourth. And then the dark fizzles into light and a girl's face fills the screen.

It's Willow. Though not as she looked on her NatterSnap picture. Instead of shiny waves, her fair hair falls in fine, straight strands, all frizzed up around the fringe. Her lips are thinner and paler than in the photo.

'Hello?' I whisper, my heart in my throat.

'Hello?' Her eyes are wide.

'Willow?' My voice trembles.

'Yes?'

'It's me, Asha.'

We stare at each other. I can't believe it's really her: my sister. My twin. Tears prick at my eyes.

'I thought you were dead,' she stammers.

121

'I know.'

She shakes her head in disbelief. 'This boy came around. Silas.'

I nod. 'I know. He wrote to me, he told me how to find you on NatterSnap.'

'He told me about you too, but he didn't explain how . . . I . . . I don't understand . . .' Her voice trails off.

Distant footsteps sound upstairs on the landing. That heavy tread sounds like Tem. I don't have much time.

'I want to meet you,' I whisper. 'I want to get away from here and find you like Silas did, but they won't let me.'

'Who won't let you?' She frowns. 'Where are you?'

'Lydia, she's in charge here. And my mum, Rose. She'll get into terrible trouble if you tell people about me.'

Willow's expression hardens and her eyes grow wary. 'Isn't Rose the one who abducted you?'

'Yes. No. She rescued me from the car crash.' I hesitate, trying to calm the panic rising inside me. 'Me being alive needs to be a secret between us. Why does anyone else need to know anyway? It's not like we have any other family.'

'What about Dad?'

I stare at her. 'Dad? What do you mean? The man who fostered you? Why would—?'

'*Our* dad,' Willow interrupts. 'Michael Hope. You just used his surname on your NatterSnap handle. Aren't you even interested in knowing him?'

The schoolroom seems to spin around me. In the distance I can hear footsteps on the stairs, but I'm glued to the spot. 'I . . . I thought our mum was on her own . . . Nobody said . . . I have a *dad*?'

WILLOW

'I have a dad?' Asha's voice is hollow, her mouth gaping.

It's really her. I don't have any doubts left. There's no way anyone could fake that mix of shock and hurt and curiosity. Adrenaline courses through my body as I peer more closely at her face, ghostly in the dim light of wherever she's standing. It's hard to make out the details – her hair and eyes are just dark smudges.

'Please tell me where you are.'

'I found a picture of the two of us.' Asha sounds like she's in a daze. 'We're on a rug and I'm in a shiny pink dress with a lilac cardigan, and you're wearing blue and looking right at me and on the back of the photo it says our names and that we're twenty months old and "Love, J, x". Have you ever seen a picture like that?'

'I don't think so,' I say. 'I'll ask my dad. Asha, he'll want to meet you. I know he will. *Please* tell me where you are.'

She shakes her head. 'I'll only tell you if you promise you won't let him call the police. Or tell anyone else at all. Okay?'

I can't see Dad going for that, but I nod anyway. 'I promise,' I say.

'Okay, then.' Asha takes a deep breath. 'I live on Dimity Island. It's—*aargh*!' The camera tilts and wobbles. Asha disappears. Thuds and scuffling noises fill the air for a second. Then the screen goes blank.

I stare at my phone. Then I snatch it up and try to call Asha back. No reply.

My thoughts run on at a hundred miles an hour. I force myself to focus. Asha is real. But she's been brainwashed and fed a load of lies. She didn't even know she has a father.

Despite all this, she wants to protect her abductors, to stop me and Dad from going to the police. And I promised her we would do what she wanted, which means Dad and I will have to find her ourselves.

I put one foot out of bed to go to him, then stop. Asha is totally real to me now, but Dad may still think I'm being conned. I need as much proof of her existence as possible before I tell him about her.

Asha said she lives on Dimity Island. Is that even a real place?

My fingers tremble as I do a search online. Dimity exists: a small, privately owned island off the south-west coast, run as a commune along 'agroecological farming principles'. I scan the information quickly. It all fits with what Asha told me — a lot of traditional farming using old-fashioned methods, like horses and ploughs instead of tractors, and very little technology. The owners are Tem and Lydia Dimity.

Asha mentioned a Lydia just now as being in charge.

I'm shivering, though it isn't particularly cold. Wrapping myself in a blanket, I get out of bed and walk over to the window. Our back garden is in total darkness, apart from a wedge of light across the patio cast from next door's first-floor window.

I don't have any doubts. Everything Asha told me was true. I go back to NatterSnap to try calling her again. I scroll up and down, but there's no longer an @AshaHope on the app.

It's as if she was never there.

Did someone delete her from NatterSnap? Was that why her call ended so abruptly — because they caught her speaking to me?

A fresh sense of dread uncoils inside me. I hurry across the landing to Dad and Becky's bedroom. The door is pulled to, but not shut. Just like always. I push it silently open a little wider and peer inside. They're fast asleep, their soft, even breathing filling the room. I crouch down beside Dad and touch his arm.

His eyes blink slowly awake. 'Willow?' he mumbles. 'What's up?'

'It's Asha,' I say. 'She just called me. It's really her.'

Dad frowns, sleepily. 'What?' He struggles onto his elbows. 'Tell me what happened.'

I explain about the DM from Silas and the video call from Asha on NatterSnap. By the time I've finished explaining everything Asha said, Becky is awake too and propped up on pillows next to Dad.

'This is preposterous,' she says. 'First someone pretending to know Asha. Now someone pretending to *be* her.'

'She wasn't pretending,' I say. 'I'm sure she wasn't.'

'Mmm.' Becky makes a face. 'These scam artists can be very convincing.'

'She's right, Willow.' Dad puts a hand on my arm.

'But why would anyone make up such a con?' I persist. 'What would they get out of it?'

'Contact with you,' Becky says immediately. She glances at Dad. 'Luring Willow into a meet-up . . . I bet that's what this Asha wanted.'

Dad raises his eyebrows. 'Is it, Willow?'

'Yes,' I admit. 'But I'm still certain she wasn't faking.'

'And yet she didn't want you telling your dad about her?' Becky's voice drips with scepticism.

'Not exactly,' I explain. 'She genuinely didn't seem to

know Dad existed. She made me promise that I could only tell Dad where she was if I was sure he wouldn't tell the police.'

Becky rolls her eyes. 'Well, that's not suspicious at all, is it?'

I bite my lip.

'So where is she?' Dad asks.

'A place called Dimity Island,' I say. 'I've looked it up online and it exists.'

'Let's see.' Dad picks up his phone and finds the same info on the island that I did. 'Anyone could read this,' he says. 'I bet she didn't give you any detailed info on it.'

'No,' I admit, 'she got cut off.'

'What did you say her name was on NatterSnap?' he asks.

'@AshaHope, but that handle's gone now.'

Dad puts on his glasses and pores over his screen.

Becky wrinkles her nose. 'Hang on. If Asha didn't know your dad existed, how come she was using his name for her NatterSnap?'

'Because it's my name too – and Mum's,' I say. 'She must have been trying to get my attention so I'd respond to her.'

It's clear from her expression that Becky isn't convinced.

'There's no @AshaHope on NatterSnap.' Dad looks up.

'I know. I already told you – it's been deleted.' My

stomach churns with anxiety. 'Don't you see? She got cut off suddenly. I think whoever interrupted her took her phone and deleted her profile.'

Dad looks at me with frustrated concern. 'Willow, listen. You *have* to let this go.'

'But—'

'None of it makes sense!' His voice rises. I can see he's really upset, though he's trying not to show it. 'Think about it. Asha makes out that she needs help to get away from this Dimity Island. Indeed, you apparently witness a sudden end of the call, reinforcing the idea she's being kept there against her will. And yet she insists that you don't involve the police.'

'She's worried her mum will get into trouble,' I say stubbornly.

'You mean the woman who abducted her?' Becky sniffs. 'The woman she also claims to want to get away from so she can meet you?'

I try to remember exactly what Asha said. 'She mentioned two women: Rose, who Silas told me about too, and who Asha thinks of as her mum; and Lydia, who runs the island. It's Lydia she's scared of.' I hesitate. 'There was a photo that Asha saw too – of her and me together at twenty months. She . . . she said I was wearing a blue dress and she was in shiny pink with a lilac cardy and we were sitting on a rug, and our mum had written our names and age on the back and "Love, J" with a kiss.' I grab Dad's hand. 'Do you remember ever seeing a picture like that, Dad?'

'I don't think so.' Dad frowns. 'Still, it is very specific.' Doubt creeps into his expression for the first time. 'Look, your uncle and aunts will be here later today. Let's talk to them, make a decision after that.'

'Come on, Willow,' Becky says, getting out from under the covers. 'Back to bed – you need to get some sleep.'

She ushers me out of the door and along the landing. Dad follows, careful to creep past the boys' room so as not to wake them up.

I get back into bed. Dad kisses my forehead. 'I'm so sorry this is happening to you, my love,' he says softly. 'Don't worry, we will get to the bottom of it.'

As he turns away, I grab his hand. 'Do you believe the girl who called me is her – Asha?' I ask.

Dad makes a face. 'Not really,' he says, 'but even a tiny percentage of doubt makes it unbearable. That's why I want to talk to the rest of the family. Now, get some rest.'

It takes a long time before I fall into an uneasy sleep, Asha's voice echoing in my head.

ASHA

Do I really have a dad? A living father? I can't get my head around it.

I sit on the sofa, numb with shock, as Tem and Lydia pace around their living room, discussing what I've done as if I wasn't there.

'Asha definitely gave the name of the island?' Lydia demands.

'Yes, I heard her!' Tem replies, his voice low and terse. 'It was the last thing she said before I knocked the phone out of her hand.'

I grimace. After Tem caught me speaking to Willow, he dragged me up here to where Lydia was already awake and pulling on a dressing gown.

Lydia turns on me. 'How could you be so stupid?' she exclaims. 'Stealing our phone and making a call behind our backs!'

'You've been going behind my back all my life!' I snap, my head clearing as my anger surges. 'You didn't just lie about Willow. You lied about me having a dad. Willow

131

just told me about him. You took me away from my *actual father.*'

Tem frowns. 'What are you talking about, Asha?'

I look at him. Is it possible that Lydia kept that detail to herself? Knowing her, it is. She is looking at me now, with an expression of deep annoyance.

'I had no idea you had a father,' Lydia insists.

'I had his *name*, Asha *Hope!*' My voice rises. 'My mum had it too. How could you not have known?'

'I read your name – and your mother's – in the news reports at the time of the accident,' Lydia says briskly. 'There was no mention of your father. How was I supposed to know your mother had a husband?'

'You were supposed to check!' I explode.

'Everything happened too fast.' Lydia holds up her hands. 'You have no idea, Asha. I was just trying to help Rose.'

'Help yourself to Rose's money, you mean,' I snap.

'How dare you make such an outrageous accusation.' Lydia says icily, clenching her fists. 'I have only ever acted in your best interests.'

'How is stealing me from my father and sister in my best interests?' I can't believe she's trying to justify it. 'You are . . . You're—' I stop, unable to think of an insult big enough.

'Excuse me,' Tem says tersely, 'but there's no point going over the past. We need to focus on the mess we're in right now.'

No point?

'Oh, this is more than a mess.' Lydia's voice rises. 'It's a *disaster*. Asha's not only made contact with her sister – she's also given her the name of this island so that Willow can find her.'

'So what do we do?' Tem demands.

'Willow won't tell the police where I am,' I pipe up. 'She promised.'

Lydia throws me a scathing look. 'Is that so?' Clearly, she doesn't believe Willow will keep her word. 'Well, we can't take any chances. We need to take precautions.'

'That's right,' Tem says. 'Everyone on the island needs to be reminded that you and Rose only bypassed the official adoption system on the mainland all those years ago because you genuinely believed Asha's best chance for the future was Rose taking her.'

'And that Rose will be sent to jail if the police find Asha now,' Lydia adds, staring meaningfully at me.

Her threat from our earlier discussion echoes in my head: '*If I go down, Rose is going down with me.*'

I glare at her. 'You're the one who belongs in jail.'

'So . . . if the police come to the island, we need to

133

keep Asha out of sight,' Lydia continues, as if I hadn't spoken.

Fear spirals inside me. 'I don't want to be locked in the storeroom like Silas.'

'No,' Lydia says. 'No, that won't work. Look, Asha, what matters is that we all carry on as normal and that you don't say *anything* to Rose or anyone else about your call to Willow.'

'Why should I do anything you tell—?'

'Do you want Rose to go to prison?' Lydia's eyebrows shoot up.

I press my lips together. Lydia seems completely convinced that Willow or our father will call the authorities, but Willow promised me she wouldn't let that happen. I've only spoken to her for two minutes, but I'm sure she won't put me in danger. If she and our dad come looking for me, I'm not going to hide away like a nasty secret.

'From now on I want to know where you are at all times,' Lydia says.

I open my mouth to object, then think better of it. The more I appear to be going along with Lydia's demands, the freer I'll be to make contact with my dad and Willow when – if – they arrive on the island.

'Okay, all that will work,' Tem says, 'so long as we

keep a watch on the jetty to spot any unexpected boats before they arrive.'

Lydia nods. 'You sort out a watch rota, Tem. I'll get the island united behind the truth.'

I snort. 'Truth?' Silas was right: Lydia is such a hypocrite.

Lydia stalks over. 'In the meantime, you need to go home, Asha.' She pauses, looming over me. 'And remember – don't tell anyone about your call with Willow, including your mother. Let me talk to Rose.'

No way am I doing what Lydia asks.

As soon as I get home, I wake Mum and tell her that I've spoken to Willow. Mum listens to my report of our conversation with an anxious expression on her face, her fingers immediately fluttering to the little crescent moon dangling from her necklace.

'So did you know?' My voice cracks. 'That I have a dad?'

Mum stares at me. 'No,' she says, her mouth gaping with horror. 'No, of *course* I didn't. I can't believe it. That poor man. What did Lydia say?'

'She *says* she didn't know he existed when you brought me here,' I say. 'But she's the one who read the news

135

reports at the time and I can't believe they didn't mention him.'

'If Lydia says she didn't know, then she didn't,' Mum says. She reaches for my hand. 'Come on, love. Lydia would never have let me take you if she knew you had a dad.'

I pull away. As usual, Mum has leaped to Lydia's defence, but I'm not at all sure she's right. Lydia lied about Willow. How can I trust that she didn't lie about me having a father?

'Lydia wants me to keep quiet about him,' I say sullenly. 'She wants me to stay here and never meet my dad and my sister.' I clench my fists. 'It's not fair.'

'I know,' Mum says. She suddenly sounds nervous. 'But if Lydia thinks that's the best thing to do, then I really think we ought to do it. I wouldn't want us to go against her.'

I shake my head. Until the last few weeks, I'd never realized just how much under Lydia's thumb Mum is. 'Why?' I demand.

Mum fidgets awkwardly, her face riddled with anxiety. 'It's just . . .' She hesitates. 'Lydia knows best,' she finishes lamely.

WILLOW

I sleep late on Saturday, waking only an hour before my cousins are due. I hurry down the stairs to find Dad in the hall, looking bleary-eyed with tiredness. Along the corridor, in the kitchen, Becky is ordering the boys to clear away their toys and help her lay the table.

Dad beckons me into the living room and shuts the door. I glance at the only remaining photo on the sideboard of me and Asha with Mum. We used to have more, but gradually they've been put away. We are little babies in the picture, just a few months old. Not like in the picture Asha described to me.

Dad clears his throat. 'We don't want to say anything about Asha in front of Billy and Ben, okay? Becky thinks hearing that she might be alive would be confusing for them.'

I nod.

'However,' Dad goes on, 'I have been on the phone to your uncle Jam and told him everything so he can fill in the others before they get here.' He pauses. 'Jam reminded me that there might have been a short window – just a few minutes – before the tide came in, when someone could have abducted Asha from the crash site.'

'That's exactly what Silas said happened, that the woman who found her – Rose – saved her life.'

'I know.' Dad blows out his breath. 'The original team of investigating officers said the tide would have come in too fast and of course the very next day Asha's empty car seat washed up down the coast, with the bindings all torn, but . . .'

'Maybe they were wrong.'

Dad nods; I can see the strain etched on his face. 'Jam still agrees with me that the most likely explanation is that the call was part of some elaborate con, but we're going to talk more when they get here. Not long now.'

'Right,' I say.

I can't help but feel that the adults are taking the situation away from me. My insides feel all churned up.

'Do . . . do you still miss Asha, Dad?' I ask.

Dad hesitates for a second. 'Yes,' he says. 'I miss her every day. Every single day.'

My two aunts and Uncle Jam, plus their partners and children, arrive in three cars. My cousins – Ellen, Jam's daughter; and Harlan, Auntie Juniper's son – emerge from the last of these and stroll up the path. They are only a few months older than me, but, if I hadn't known them all my life, I'd find them super intimidating. Ellen's skin has a beautifully natural glow; she has on the lightest flick of mascara and lip gloss, a perfectly fitting red dress and isn't wearing any jewellery. Harlan, on the other hand, is dressed from head to toe in black with a row of chunky rings on his fingers and dark licks of eyeliner over his eyes. They both look effortlessly cool.

'Hey, cuz!' Harlan says shyly.

'Hi!' I say, trying to smile back. 'You okay?'

'We're fine.' Ellen rushes up and envelops me in a hug. 'But never mind us. I overheard Dad telling Mum that you've had a call from your dead sister!'

'Ellie.' Harlan prods her arm. 'Could you *be* any more insensitive?'

'Sorry,' Ellen says, pulling back and wincing. 'But it just sounds so crazy.'

'It is,' I say. 'Come on, I'll tell you upstairs.'

The three of us hurry up to my room. Becky made me tidy up yesterday and it feels lighter and airier than usual. Sunshine streams in through the open window, bouncing off the huge disco ball on my desk and sending tiny dots of bright silver light across the wall. Ellen plonks herself in the middle of my bed, her long legs folded under her. Harlan perches next to her.

'Go on – what happened?' Ellen urges, leaning forward.

'Give her a chance.' Harlan frowns.

This is how they always are, how they've been since we were little: Ellen in charge and Harlan smoothing the rough edges off her bossy behaviour. The two of them weren't just born within a couple of weeks of each other, but within a few streets too. They go to the same school and are, as far as I can tell, each other's best friend, more like brother and sister than cousins. Last year they nearly died after getting trapped together in a disused quarry and, since then, they've been closer than ever.

Maybe, if I hadn't lost Asha when we were tiny, she and I would have been like that?

The thought lodges in me like a thorn in the throat.

'You do look super stressed, Willow,' Harlan adds, his dark eyes full of sympathy. 'But if you don't want to talk, it's fine.'

'No, I do,' I say.

I tell my cousins the whole story. As I finish, Becky calls us downstairs. I move to the door, but neither Ellen nor Harlan follows. Instead they both stare at me, real shock in their eyes.

'What?' I ask.

140

'That is the most *insane* story I've ever heard,' Ellen says at last.

I swallow, hard. 'But do you think it's true?'

'Why would someone make it up?' Harlan asks.

'I don't know,' Ellen says, 'but . . . but it *can't* be true. How on earth could a missing child stay hidden for twelve years?'

'Easily enough, if no one's looking for them,' I point out. 'And no one would be looking, if everyone thought they were dead.'

Suddenly, I very much want my cousins to believe in Asha.

'Hey, teenagers!' Becky's shout is fiercer than before. 'Downstairs, now!'

Ellen and Harlan finally stand up and we go downstairs.

The grown-ups are waiting for us around the kitchen table. I glance at Dad. His face is drawn and haggard. I stand beside him, waiting for him to speak. At last he clears his throat. 'Your uncle has brought something to show you.'

At this, Uncle Jam reaches into his bag, pulls out a photograph album and offers it to me. 'Look at the picture on page four,' he says softly.

I take the album and open it up. The photos on the first page are all of Ellen, when she was a baby. I turn the stiff card to the second and third pages. Most of the pictures are still of her, of course, but there are some of Harlan and me and Asha too. I reach the fourth page.

There it is: the photo of me and Asha in party dresses on a rug, exactly as Asha described it to me last night. I'm dressed in blue; Asha in pink with a lilac cardigan. My fingers tremble as I take the photo out and turn it over. There's nothing written on the back.

'Is this the picture Asha told you about?' Dad asks.

'Yes.' I look at Uncle Jam. 'How did you get it?'

'Actually, I *took* it,' Uncle Jam says. 'I got a copy done for your mum so she could frame it. I hadn't thought about it, but I gave it to her the day she died. She'd been to visit with Asha.'

'That's right,' Dad says. 'You were at home with me, Willow, because you'd had a cold.'

I nod, impatiently. Dad has told me that last detail many times. 'Go on, Uncle Jam.'

He frowns, remembering. 'I gave Jasmine a copy of this picture and she put it in Asha's baby bag. Insofar as I ever thought about it, I guess I assumed it was destroyed in the car crash.'

My voice shakes. 'Asha said that on the version she had, there was some writing on the back, something like: "*Asha and Willow – twenty months*. Love, J" with a kiss after.'

142

Uncle Jam nods. 'That was me. I took the picture on Ellen's birthday. Like I say, I just did the one copy for Jasmine.' He hands it to me. 'Here, take it.'

So it was *J* for Jam, not Jasmine. I take the picture and look up. Everyone around the table is staring at us. Dad's face is ashen.

'Is there any way anyone would know about this picture?' he asks Uncle Jam.

'No, this is the only other print and it's been in this album for twelve years,' Jam said.

'It's never left the house before,' Lauren adds. 'And there's certainly no way anyone would know what Jam wrote on the back of the only copy.'

'So how did the girl who called me last night get hold of that copy?' I ask, slowly.

I meet Dad's gaze.

'It's not proof,' he says. 'But . . .' He hesitates. 'Oh, God . . . Asha.' As Dad speaks, his voice cracks and he sniffs back what I am almost certain is a tear. He turns away, clearly not wanting anyone to see. 'Sorry, everyone,' he says gruffly.

'We're all upset,' Uncle Jam says.

'Exactly,' adds Becky, putting her arm across Dad's shoulders.

I stare at him. I've been so wrapped up in my own

concerns, I haven't really thought about how it must be for Dad to find out that the daughter he thought he lost twelve years ago might still be alive.

I glance outside. Dark clouds are gathering in the sky.

Dad blows out his breath and turns back to the table. He stands up. 'I'm going to call the police,' he says. 'Get them to go to Dimity Island and see if Asha is there.'

'But Asha said *not* to call the police.' I jump up.

'That doesn't make sense, Willow. Come on, we don't know anything about the people on this island. If Asha really is there, she could be in danger.' Dad frowns. 'Surely you can see we need to get the authorities involved.'

'Your dad's right,' Uncle Jam says.

More murmurs of consent ripple around the table. I glance over at Harlan and Ellen. They're both watching intently. Ellen has an expression of deep shock on her face.

'But I *promised* her,' I say, my guts twisting.

'This is serious, Willow,' Dad says. 'If this girl *is* Asha . . .' His voice breaks on her name; then he clears his throat. 'Calling the police is our only option.'

I can tell from his tone there's no point arguing. Dad might be the gentlest man you'll ever meet, but when he makes a decision, he sticks to it. So I sit back down, my stomach churning with worry, and Dad makes the call.

ASHA

After speaking to Willow for the first time *and* finding out I have a dad, there's no way I can get excited for tonight's stupid spring equinox party. I know it's supposed to be a community-wide celebration for all the springtime birthdays on the island, including – thanks to Mum trying to do something special for me – my own, but getting excited about either birthdays or parties now seems as pointless and childish to me as all the other things I used to 'ooh' and 'ahh' about on the island.

Mum doesn't get this, of course. She and Pixie are elbow-deep in preparations: Mum is sorting out flowers while Pixie sews triangles of colourful cloth to hang up as bunting in the Community Room. Lydia came round at breakfast and spoke privately to Mum. Since then Mum has deliberately avoided any mention of either Willow or my dad, and when, after Lydia went, I tried to talk to her and Pixie about them, Mum insisted I stopped, with a truly terrified look on her face.

None of this has stopped me thinking about them,

endless questions careering around my head: What has Willow done since we spoke last night? Is she going to talk to our dad and come and find me here? How will Tem and Lydia react if they show up?

And they *will* show up – won't they?

I'm certain Willow wants to meet me. And if my dad feels anything like I do, he must surely want to know me too. Mustn't he?

But when will they come? And how? Tem has organized a patrol to look out for boats. Winston Rickett and his daughter, Jemma, are on the jetty now, while the island's chief carpenter, Harry Smith, who keeps himself to himself most of the time, has volunteered to keep watch during the party.

I try to focus on my household chores, fetching a brush and sweeping out the grate in the living room. Mum wanders outside to rake our potato patch.

'Hey, Asha!' Pixie calls from across the room. She's brought over her sewing machine and set it up in the corner. 'Look!' She holds up her dress fabric and the blue darkens as the light shifts on it. 'I'm making a dress for myself just like the one I made for you, only yours is green and mine is blue!'

'That's lovely,' I say, smiling. Pixie has seemed much more cheerful since showing me Silas's letter. I guess she must be relieved that he's safe with family.

'Oooh, I almost forgot!' Pixie squeals with excitement and rushes over to the big wooden chest under the window, where Mum has let her put some of her clothes. She rummages around and finally draws out a soft pale green jacket. 'I hardly ever wear this, but I thought you might like to borrow it, for over your dress?'

'Thank you.' I take the jacket and make a show of trying it on and saying how nice it is. Pixie chatters away about the darts she's putting into her dress. I can't really follow the detail of what she's saying – my own clothes-making experience doesn't extend much beyond sewing basics like hems and repairs.

'I modelled our dresses on this one I saw on the mainland when we visited a few years ago, before they had that plague thing,' Pixie burbles. 'All those shops were *full* of clothes. Can you imagine?'

I can't really, though I've seen pictures of clothes shops, and in school Lydia has told us how they're part of the western world's economic model, how much pollution fast fashion causes *and* what a destructive effect it can have on people, encouraging them to obsess about their appearance.

But maybe Lydia's got that wrong. Maybe she's lying about the outside world just like she lied about Silas pushing her and, I'm certain, lied about knowing my dad existed.

I take off the jacket, my thoughts turning again to Willow.

What is she doing right now? How long will it take her to organize a trip to the island? How urgently will she and our dad act?

A few hours later and the sun is low in the sky as Mum, Pixie and I stroll along the lane to Dimity House. The solar lights along the path send out a dim glow into the dusk while the evening wind bites at my cheeks, whipping up the sea around the island. The land slopes downhill as the three of us round the bend in the lane. Dimity House comes into view, with the beach, sea and jetty beyond it. It looks its best at this time of night – the grandest house on the island, the only one made of brick. The last rays of sunlight glint off the roof, while fairy lights sparkle from inside the Community Room. The faint sound of Sally Brickman's fiddle-playing drifts across the evening air.

'Ooh, dancing!' Mum cries, clasping her hands together.

'I can't wait!' adds Pixie.

As I follow them into the warm air of the Community Room to lay our potluck dishes on the table, a buzz runs round the room. I grimace. I can't hear what they're saying, but from the way people are looking over, then very obviously looking away again, I am the main topic of conversation. I stand, feeling self-conscious, in front of the table. Pushed back against the wall, it is laden with platters of cheese and quiche and rolls and a big tureen of steaming soup. I sniff the scent of leek and potato, trying to calm down.

Our school teacher Max and his partner, Jacob, wave at me from beside the fire that crackles in the huge grate opposite. I wave back, then notice Chola Rickett – looking very unlike herself in a long, silky skirt – chatting to Tem on the other side of the fire. Just beyond them, Pixie has joined Jemma Rickett, who is organizing the smaller kids into some kind of charades game. Sally Brickman's grandson Aaron is now accompanying her fiddle-playing on his guitar: a lively tune I don't recognize skips and bounces around the room. The air is warm and heavy with the scent of someone's flowery perfume.

'A quick word, Asha?' It's Lydia. I jump as she hisses in my ear.

'What?' I ask, scowling at her.

'I've told everyone that the authorities on the mainland are challenging the way Rose adopted you and that some people may come to the island asking about you.' She purses her lips.

149

So that's why everyone in the room is staring at me. 'Are you serious?'

'Deadly,' Lydia says.

'Did you tell people about my dad? About Willow?'

'Absolutely not,' Lydia snaps. 'And I'll thank you to keep quiet about them.'

I meet her gaze. 'You mean lie?'

Lydia rolls her eyes. 'It's hardly a lie to say nothing,' she says. 'Plus *all* of this is to protect Rose.'

'And you,' I point out.

'Oh, please.' Lydia gives an impatient tut and stalks off. I stand, feeling very alone in the crowded room.

Mum and Annie wander closer. 'That's wonderful news,' Mum is saying, clutching the crescent moon around her neck, and pushing the point of the curved tip into her hand. 'Did you hear, Asha? Eva is pregnant again.'

'Oh,' I say. 'Great.'

'Are you all right?' Mum asks anxiously, as Annie melts away.

I shake my head. 'It's Lydia,' I say. 'She's making up stories and—'

'Please just do what she says, Asha.' Mum gulps. '*Please.*'

I stare at her, tears suddenly pricking at my eyes. The most important moment of my life happened last night, when I spoke to my sister for the first time and found out

I have a real, live dad. And yet I'm not allowed to talk to anyone about it.

I've never felt more like an outsider than I do right now.

The musicians are playing a strathspey for everyone to dance to. The sounds of laughter and wild strings wash over us.

'The Eightsome Reel will be next,' Mum says. 'Shall we dance it, Asha?'

Instead of replying, I hurry away across the room. As I reach the door, I glance over my shoulder. Mum is now deep in conversation with Lydia. She's nodding, fiddling anxiously with that necklace of hers again. She looks terrified, just like she did after Lydia's visit this morning. A dark fury rises inside me. Everything bad that has happened to me, from losing my birth family, to Silas running away from the island, to being the unwanted focus of attention tonight – it's all Lydia's fault.

As the music stops and Sally calls out the next dance, I slip out into the hall and then through the back, onto the porch where, just two weeks and one day ago, I watched Silas escape on the supply boat. The night air hits me – fresh and cool and carrying the scent of the sea. I make my way down to the beach, the wind picking up as I leave the shelter of the house. I'm cold now, without my coat, but it's peaceful here. I can't believe how much my life has changed in such a short space of time. Knowing that I have a dad and a sister changes everything.

Lights wink on the horizon. I look up, peering out to sea.

It's a boat. Yes, definitely a boat. My heart lurches into my throat. Surely it's them, Willow and our father? They've come for me and they'll talk to Mum and Lydia and everyone will find a way to deal with the new situation we're in, but, above everything else, I'll have a new family to find out about and, maybe, one day feel close to.

The crackle of radio static drifts across the air from the jetty. I peer in that direction, in time to see a dark figure passing the main jetty light. It's Harry Smith on lookout.

I can make out the low mumble of his voice, but not what he's saying.

The door behind me slams open. Tem and Lydia burst onto the porch.

'Here she is!' Lydia says, spotting me.

'Are you sure?' Tem is speaking into his radio.

Harry Smith's reply rings out. 'Yes,' he says, 'it's the police. Small boat. Just two men in uniform on board.'

Police?

'They didn't waste any time,' Lydia mutters, grabbing

my arm. 'Right, you deal with the officers, Tem.'

'What are—?' I start.

'Will do!' Tem hurries off.

Lydia tightens her grip on my arm. 'Come with me, Asha.' She drags me away, around the side of the house.

I take the first few steps without thinking. I'm too shocked that the police are almost at the island. Then I stop and pull away. Could Willow and my dad be with them somehow? Lydia tugs at me again, but I hold my ground.

'Where are we going?' I demand.

'To make sure the police don't find you,' Lydia says.

'But . . .' My head spins.

'There's no "but" about it,' Lydia says. 'The police *have* to leave here convinced that no one called Asha lives on Dimity Island. Everyone on the island knows it. You know it too. Otherwise Rose goes to jail.'

'But what about my sister and my dad?' I look towards the boat.

'You heard Harry on the radio: the only people on board are two uniformed men,' Lydia says, leading me around the side of the house.

'But—?'

Lydia stops and gives me a shake. 'Don't you understand, Asha? Your precious sister has broken her promise to you, just like I said she would. She's told your dad you're alive

153

and he's obviously gone straight to the authorities.'

I stare at her, my heart thudding.

'What happens next is up to you,' Lydia goes on. 'Either we find a good hiding place for you until the police leave, or you make a fuss and they find you.' She pauses to give her next words maximum effect. 'And if they find you, I will make sure that you'll be taken away from Rose forever and she'll go to jail.'

I stare at her, speechless with fury. She's putting me in an impossible position.

'So?' Lydia says. 'What are you going to do?'

WILLOW

It's midnight, but though Auntie Jade and her family have gone, everyone else remains huddled around the kitchen table. This is mostly thanks to Harlan and Ellen – who flatly refused to leave me until news came about Asha.

After all the earlier talking, the house is weirdly quiet. Billy is, at last, asleep, while Becky is upstairs with Ben, who, sensing the disturbed atmosphere in the house, can't seem to settle down.

I know how he feels. According to the latest phone call to Dad, the police have put out an alert to find Silas in order to question him *and* sent two officers in a boat to the island. They should be there by now, searching for Asha.

I can't stop wondering what she'll think when they turn up. I promised her I wouldn't let Dad contact the authorities, and yet that's exactly what he's done. A creeping sensation wriggles uncomfortably under my skin. I don't want to face it, but the truth is I've broken the very first promise I made to my twin.

'What I don't understand,' says Auntie Juniper with a

frown, 'is why – if it really is Asha – she hasn't tried to leave the island herself. Surely there must be a way off it?'

Everyone looks at me.

'She said she tried to leave with Silas, the boy who came to the house,' I explain. 'Something went wrong.'

'It's not that easy to leave,' Dad adds. 'The island's pretty cut off. A supply boat visits every other Friday, but that's it.'

'But it's an *island*,' Uncle Jam points out. 'Surely plenty of the people who live there have their own boats?'

'I don't know.' Dad wrings his hands. He looks like he's aged ten years in the past ten hours. 'I just don't know.'

The other adults murmur sympathetically. Auntie Juniper pats Dad's arm gently. 'We'll know soon en—'

Dad's phone rings, blasting into the quiet of the kitchen. He snatches it up, his skin pale under the electric lights as he listens to the person on the other end. I stare at his face, trying to read his expression. After less than a minute, Dad puts down his phone.

'They didn't find Asha.' He sighs heavily. 'Apparently nobody on the island has ever heard of her.'

'Oh, goodness!' Auntie Juniper gasps.

'Well, that's a blow, but also a relief,' Uncle Jam says. 'I couldn't bear the thought of her imprisoned on an island and away from us all these years.'

My head spins. Dad lets out a sigh.

'Ah, well,' he says sorrowfully, 'the whole story never did make sense.'

I stare at him. Is he just going to accept what the police say? That the Asha who called me was a fraud?

'I think it makes less sense that Willow was totally scammed,' Ellen says. 'What about the photo? How did the scammers get hold of that?'

Harlan wrinkles his nose. 'Yeah, and what were they thinking they'd get out of Willow by pretending Asha was alive?'

Dad and Uncle Jam exchange a glance.

'Let's not dwell on that,' Jam says.

'But the people in charge on the island could have hidden Asha somewhere,' I point out. 'She *told* me not to call the police.'

'I'm sure the police did a thorough search,' Dad says, patting my hand. 'Now, time for bed, Willow.'

I can't believe it.

I sit, stunned, at the kitchen table as everyone else rises, gathering coats and saying quiet goodbyes. Becky reappears and joins the general consensus that the whole episode has been a horrible, nightmarish blip in our lives and that it's important we all put it behind us as soon as possible.

157

They're talking as if it's happening to all of them, equally. But it isn't. It's mainly happening to me. I'm the sister. I'm the one Asha called.

I'm the only person who spoke to either her or Silas.

And now, no one believes what I saw and heard was real.

Ellen and Harlan come over to say goodbye. I hug them in a daze.

'I don't believe it was a hoax,' Ellen whispers.

'Me neither,' adds Harlan.

I nod, too choked up to speak. It means a lot to have them on my side, but what difference does it make? I'm as far away from finding Asha as ever.

ASHA

Time ticks slowly past. I'm cramped and chilled to the bone. Lydia has hidden me in the boat shelter. I'm under a blanket in the storage box, behind the petrol canisters.

After several hours in here, I'm stiff with cold, but I daren't climb out. Lydia made it clear that if I identified myself to the police, she would ensure Rose took the fall for abducting me. I can't bear the idea that Mum might go to jail, least of all because of something I've done.

I keep listening out for the sound of the police coming by, but the island is deathly quiet, the only noise the occasional caw of a distant bird. At last I hear footsteps, then Lydia's low, triumphant voice just outside the box.

'We did it,' she says, lifting the lid.

I climb out, rubbing my arms up and down. The boat shelter is dark, lit only by Lydia's electric lantern. Across the rocks, the motorboat Silas wanted to steal all those weeks ago bobs on the water inside the metal cage Tem constructed.

'Have the police gone?' I ask. 'I didn't hear them.'

'Yes – they went round to most of the cottages, but everyone backed me to the hilt and denied any knowledge of you, so they only gave this bit of the coastline a cursory search.' She pauses. 'You did well, Asha. Very well.'

I turn away. Lydia's praise is the last thing I want. We walk back to my cottage in silence. Lydia leaves me at the door. Mum sweeps me into a hug as soon as I walk in. She chatters away, concerned that I'm cold, that I was frightened.

She doesn't get it at all.

The only thing I feel is let down.

I trusted Willow to make sure the police didn't come after Mum – and she betrayed me. I hate to admit it, but Lydia was right about that.

Willow lied. Lydia lied. I'm surrounded by lies.

The next eleven days pass in a blur. I have fallen into a slump that nothing seems to rouse me from. Mum tries to talk to me about the garden and the hens and how well Edison the goat has adapted to living in our yard, while Pixie attempts to interest me in the latest outfit she's planning.

Nothing works. It's not that I have time on my hands. Lydia has kept me busy with extra daily tasks in the

160

kitchen: scrubbing the big ovens and spring-cleaning every cupboard. I'm on a tight leash, for sure. But that's not the worst of it. In some subtle way, everyone on the island looks at me differently. Of course, a lot of them have known for a long time that Rose adopted me without going through all the proper legal procedures. I'm sure Lydia convinced them they'd had no choice, back when I arrived on the island twelve years ago. But nobody had talked about it for such a long time that the subject was half forgotten. Until now.

Lydia has given me strict instructions to avoid the whole subject – and I'm sure she's asked everyone not to talk to me about it too. But an awareness is still there in their gaze: from the pity and sorrow of Samira Asiki and Sally Brickman, to the anxious worry of the Ricketts' and Lydia herself.

After a lifetime of never questioning my position on Dimity Island, I feel like I don't belong. Not that I have any way of leaving. As I saw when I was hiding from the police, the motorboat – which is the only boat on the island that could do the journey to the mainland – is locked away inside a metal cage.

Anyway, even if I could find a way to the mainland, there's nothing for me there.

Willow betrayed me. She broke her promise to keep

me a secret – and to make our dad keep me a secret. Whichever way I look at it, I can't help but feel that I don't mean as much to her as I'd hoped.

And that is the worst feeling I've ever had.

WILLOW

Today is a half day. Normally a free afternoon would see me out with my friends but, as I've told Dad several times, I just want to be home alone at the moment. I get home from school just before 1 p.m. and go straight upstairs to change out of my uniform. I fling open my wardrobe and the clothes stare back at me, the usual jumbled mess. I select a pair of jeans.

Would Asha wear jeans? What other clothes might she like? I smooth back a strand of fine, frizzy hair. Asha's hair was all dark with natural curls. Sooo pretty.

It's been like this for the past eleven days. No matter how much I try to put her out of my head – like Dad said I should – Asha haunts me. Whatever I do, everything comes back to her. At school, I wonder if she's ever had lessons and what they were like. At home, I find myself imagining what kind of house she lives in. Eating dinner, I think about the food she would eat on her island. Because, whatever Dad says, I have no doubt that Asha is real. My long-lost twin sister. She said she wanted to leave – to meet me and Dad in person – and I messed everything up.

I don't know what to do now. I unblocked Silas on NatterSnap several days ago and sent him my number and the following message:

I believe you about Asha. I'm sorry, please call me

There seemed no point asking him to talk to the police, not after everything that's happened. He was as adamant as Asha that I shouldn't tell anyone she was alive. I just want to talk to him again.

But Silas hasn't responded.

All I know is that somehow, some way, I am going to find Asha myself. I've spent hours going over the long trip I'd need to make to get to Salthaven, the small town on the coast nearest to the island. From there, maybe, I can hire a boat.

But it will cost a lot. And I have precisely £22.79 to my name.

I pull a jumper on over my T-shirt and turn away from the mirror. The doorbell goes. Dad and Becky are still at work, so I pad downstairs and open the door. Ellen and Harlan are standing on the step. Ellen is wearing jeans and a red jacket and has a backpack slung over her shoulder. Harlan is dressed in black, as usual, one ear full of silver earrings and a small holdall in his hand.

'Hey, cuz.' Harlan raises his hand, smiling at the look of shock on my face.

'Hey.' I turn from him to Ellen, feeling baffled. 'Er, what are you guys doing here?'

They exchange a glance.

'Can we come in?' Ellen asks. 'I'm dying of thirst. We've been travelling since first thing this morning.'

'We skipped school, got the Tube across town, then a whole bunch of buses,' Harlan adds.

'To . . . to come here?' I stammer, standing back to let them pass. 'To see me?'

'Yeah, your dad told mine that you'd be at home on your own this afternoon. I think he's a bit worried about you.' Ellen grimaces. 'We thought we'd get here sooner, to be honest. It was much easier when we came by car, with the parents.'

'Yeah, you kind of live in the middle of nowhere, Willow.' Harlan chuckles.

I lead them along the hall and into the kitchen, my head spinning.

'Did you really ditch a whole day at school?' I ask, as I pour them each a glass of water.

Harlan nods, sitting down at the table.

'But . . . but *why*?'

Harlan glances at Ellen, then takes a gulp of water.

'Harlan and I both think Asha is still alive,' Ellen says, joining Harlan at the table. She looks me in the eye. 'We reckon the adults just can't face the truth.'

Harlan grunts. 'Not exactly that . . . More that they can't believe it's true. It's too big a shift.'

'Whatever,' Ellen says. 'The point is, we think you're right about Asha. That you've been right all along.'

'Exactly,' Harlan adds.

I gaze from her to Harlan, a lump forming in my throat.

'Thank you,' I say.

'There's more.' Harlan raises his eyebrows.

'I can't live knowing that Asha is out there,' Ellen goes on. 'I have to *do* something.'

'As usual,' Harlan murmurs under his breath.

Ellen nudges him with her elbow, but doesn't take her eyes off me.

'I want to do something too,' I say. 'But I don't have enough money.'

'That's where we come in,' Ellen says. 'We're going to help you find Asha.'

My jaw drops.

'If that's what *you* want,' Harlan adds hurriedly.

'It is! I've been thinking about it since I saw you, but—'

'We've got nearly two hundred pounds between us.' Harlan holds up his wallet.

'Which should be plenty to get the three of us to Dimity Island,' Ellen says, grinning.

I grip the edge of the kitchen table, unable to believe it. 'Are you serious?'

'Of course,' Ellen says. 'You just need to grab a jumper, put some things in a bag.'

'I've sorted the cheapest bus routes,' says Harlan.

'And once we get to Salthaven,' Ellen goes on, 'we're going to try and get a ride on the supply boat that leaves from there tomorrow.'

'We reckon they shouldn't charge us much, seeing as they're going to the island anyway,' Harlan adds.

I nod, eagerly, then remember that the plan rests on us running off now and spending the night away from home. 'This all sounds great, but . . .' I frown. 'My dad will freak if I disappear.'

'We know.' Ellen waves her hand dismissively. 'All our parents will freak. But your dad won't find out unless he has some way of tracking you.' She rolls her eyes, as if to suggest what an outrageous invasion of privacy this would be. My face flushes as I remember Dad's insistence on installing that locator app on his mobile so he could track my whereabouts. Thank goodness I disabled it the other day. I take out my own phone and double-check that the location function is turned off there too.

'You just need to make out you're staying at a friend's tonight,' Ellen goes on. 'Me and Harlan have already said we'll be at each other's place – nobody will realize we've gone till we don't turn up to school tomorrow morning, and by then we'll be halfway to the island. So?' She raises her eyebrows. 'Are you up for this?'

I don't hesitate, though my heart is thumping. 'Yes,' I say. 'Yes, I am.'

We set off straight away. The first part of our journey goes remarkably smoothly. Harlan has geeked out on researching every detail of our route, while Ellen does the talking, paying cash for our return bus tickets and even managing to forage some free (and only slightly stale) rolls from a cafe where we stop to fill up our water bottles.

I send Dad a text saying that I've gone to my friend Mandeep's to work on a school project and that her mum has asked me to stay for dinner. I'll message later to ask if it's okay for me to stay over – so that we can get up early and keep working. I've stayed at Mandeep's house lots of times, so, with luck, Dad won't realize that I didn't go there until I'm a no-show at school tomorrow.

It's six thirty, early evening, and, after travelling for almost five hours on several different buses, we're due at Salthaven in twenty minutes. The bus we're on now is small, hot and stuffy – though thankfully almost empty. I'm sitting with our bags next to me; Ellen and Harlan share the seat behind. I stare out of the window at the passing fields. After a sunny day, the clouds are gathering, dark grey and threatening rain.

Harlan has found us a place to stay in Salthaven. It's cheap, so far as accommodation goes, but will take a big chunk of our funds. Still, it means that tomorrow morning we'll be right by the harbour where the supply boat sets off for Dimity Island. The bus trundles around a bend in the road and the sea comes into view below us. It spreads out like liquid steel, the white tips of the waves shimmering across its surface.

'Looks choppy,' Harlan says with a grunt. 'Like a storm's brewing.'

I glance back at him, immediately worried. 'Do you think it might mean the supply boat won't go out tomorrow?'

Harlan shrugs. 'I don't think so. Anyway, the storm will probably blow itself out by then.'

'We're not going to let a few waves stop us.' Ellen grins.

I force a smile back, then glance at my phone again,

where Dad has messaged a thumbs-up in response to my text about going to Mandeep's house after school.

Anxiety coils around my heart. I'm getting so close. I sneak a look at my face in my phone. My skin looks awful, all pale and blotchy, and my hair is frizzing up in the warm, moist air of the bus. I wish I'd remembered to bring a hairbrush or some hairclips or something.

The road winds inland and we lose sight of the sea as we drive into Salthaven. It's shabby and rundown – not what I was expecting at all – full of long rows of terraced houses with crumbling walls, and weeds growing through the pavement. The bus pulls up outside a shopping centre – all the shops are boarded over, with torn and faded flyers on the walls. We get off and look around as the bus drives away. A fierce wind has whipped up, blowing damp, salty air in our faces. The sea must be close by.

'Which way to the harbour?' Ellen asks.

'Down there.' Harlan points to our right. 'It's just a few streets away.' He frowns. 'Who are they?'

A small knot of teenagers – boys – are crossing the road, coming towards us. None of them looks friendly.

'Let's get out of here,' Ellen urges.

I turn, suddenly afraid. But the boys are running, pounding along the pavement towards us. 'Get them!' A loud cry.

I try to run, but they're on top of us. Scornful. Laughing. Surrounding us.

'Where you from?'

'Got any cash on you?'

'What you doing here?'

One of the guys knocks into me, ramming my side. I spin around, winded and furious, to see which one it is, but I can't tell. There are too many faces. Staring. Threatening. Terrifying. Suddenly I'm surrounded, hands tugging at my bag.

'Get off!' I yell.

'Hey!' That's Ellen's voice. She can't be more than a metre away from me, but I can't see her through the throng. Panic rises inside me. I grip my bag tightly. All around me is a tangle of pumping arms and legs.

'Stop!' Harlan is shouting.

'Help!' I cry.

Voices rise around me for a second; then all of a sudden it's over.

The boys are running up the road, in the opposite direction from the harbour. I look down. My bag is still in my hands. Ellen and Harlan are standing, gasping for breath, on either side of me.

'Are you okay?' Ellen asks, clutching her backpack.

'I think so,' I say.

'I'm not.' Harlan's voice is grim. Serious.

We stare at him.

'What is it?' I ask.

'One of them grabbed the cash in my pocket,' Harlan says, bitterly. 'It's gone. The money to pay for our bed and breakfast – and the boat tomorrow. It's all gone.'

I stare at Harlan, feeling sick. 'They took *all* the money?'

Ellen clutches her forehead. 'What are we going to do?' she shrieks.

'Not panic,' Harlan says firmly, though his own face has drained of colour and his eyes are darting about, clearly still worried that the boys who attacked us will come back. 'We should go to the police.'

'No,' I say. 'We can't do that without giving away why we're here. It will take too long and they might stop us.'

'Let's get down to the harbour,' Ellen urges. 'We can decide what to do and at least it will be away from here.'

We set off along the street Harlan indicated earlier.

'Maybe we can get the people who own the supply boat to take us to Dimity Island anyway,' I suggest.

'Without paying them?' Ellen raises her eyebrows.

'I still have a bit of money.' I fish for the two ten–pound notes in my pocket and hold them out, feeling desperate.

'Don't flash it around!' Ellen puts her hand over the cash.

Harlan snorts. 'They're going to want more than that.

172

And what about the bed and breakfast? How will we pay for that?'

'There *must* be a way,' I insist. I stare at Ellen, knowing that Harlan will follow her lead. Surely she won't give up. 'We've come this far.' My voice cracks. 'Please?'

'Okay, let's try.' Ellen blows out her breath. 'The priority is that boat. We can sleep outside if we have to, but we need the boat to take us to the island.'

'Let's find it then,' I urge. 'It's bound to be moored in the harbour. We just have to get the owners to agree to take us.'

Ellen and Harlan exchange a look. Harlan nods.

'Come on, then,' says Ellen.

We turn the corner and the little harbour comes into view. It's just as rundown as the rest of Salthaven, with a few shops on the right – mostly boarded up – and a crumbling stone jetty on the left. About ten boats are moored here. A couple are tiny rowing boats. The rest are bigger: some with nets slung over the deck – they must be fishing boats – and others with small cabins. Almost all of them have paint peeling from the hulls.

'How do we know which is the supply boat?' I ask, my heart sinking.

'I'll find out.' Ellen strides towards a pair of old men sitting on a bench in front of a fishing tackle shop. As I

173

watch her talking to them, Harlan leans against a wall and blows out his breath. He looks completely overwhelmed. I turn to him, feeling guilty.

'I'm so sorry about your money,' I say. 'I promise I'll pay it all back.'

'It's not that,' Harlan says. 'That attack really freaked me out.'

I nod, unsure what to say.

A moment later, Ellen comes hurrying back. She beckons us towards the stone jetty. 'I found out the name of the supply boat,' she exclaims. 'It's called *The Cutter* and the men I spoke to reckon at least one of the owners should be working on it right now.'

My heart gives a leap. 'Brilliant,' I say.

The three of us make our way up and down the first stone jetty, peering at each boat in turn. *The Cutter* is at the end of the row and probably the smartest boat moored here. Its name glints brightly: white paint against the black of the hull. A man in overalls is bent over the hatch on the deck. His fair hair gleams in the sunlight as he hammers a nail into a side piece of wood.

'Hello?' I say, feeling awkward. 'Is this your boat?'

'Yes! I'm Kieran, one of the owners.' Kieran looks up, smiling. He raises his free hand in greeting. 'What can I do for you?'

I hesitate, trying to work out what to say; how to sound as persuasive as possible.

'We need to get to Dimity Island,' Ellen says, 'and we know you're going there tomorrow. Can we come too, please?'

I cringe. Her tone is all wrong – she sounds like she's ordering this man to take us, which I can't imagine will go down well.

Sure enough, Kieran's smile vanishes. 'Why would you want to go to Dimity?' he asks slowly.

'Personal reasons,' Ellen says quickly.

'Our cousin lives there,' Harlan adds.

'Please,' I say, my cheeks burning with embarrassment that Ellen has sounded so haughty. 'It's really important we get there.'

'I'm afraid we can't take you,' Kieran says.

'Why not?' Ellen steps forward. There's an arrogant tinge to her voice now. My heart sinks. That's not going to help.

Kieran frowns. 'Well, for one thing, we don't take passengers. And definitely not kids.'

'We have a little cash,' Ellen argues.

'Yes,' I say, tugging the twenty pounds out of my pocket and holding it out. 'It's all we've got. Some boys mugged us.'

'I'm sorry.' Kieran shakes his head. 'It's not about the money. It's just not what we do.'

He turns his back and resumes his hammering. Ellen and Harlan mutter under their breath to each other. I just stand, staring at the boat. I can't believe we've come all this way, only to have our hopes dashed at the last moment. I gaze up and down *The Cutter*. The deck is already full of boxes, loosely covered by a green tarpaulin, whose side flaps in the wind. A gust sweeps over the boat, lifting one edge of the tarp up and slapping it back down again. Kieran moves instinctively to fasten it, tugging the attached rope taut.

He looks at me with a rueful smile. 'I really am sorry,' he says. 'But we can't take you.' There's a finality to his words that reminds me of Dad when he's made up his mind about something.

'Come on.' Harlan tugs at my sleeve and I let him pull me away.

The three of us trudge away along the jetty, back to where the harbour meets the road.

'I'm so sorry, Willow,' Ellen says. 'This has been a complete waste of time.'

Tears prick at my eyes. The street leading back to the bus stop stretches ahead of us, as the hum of a passing car fills the air for a second. Then silence, apart from the distant creaking of the boats in the harbour.

'We have to go home,' Ellen says.

I stare at her. 'No.'

'There's not really another option,' Harlan adds more gently. 'Especially after losing all our money.'

'But—'

'We're not giving up,' Ellen insists. 'We'll get more money from somewhere, hire our own boat. Asha will still be on the island. But today's been a total disaster and there's no point pretending it hasn't.'

I blink away the tears that are now bubbling over, a lump lodging itself in my throat. It's all very well for Ellen to suggest trying again another time, but I need to find Asha *now*.

'The last bus tonight leaves in five minutes,' Harlan says, looking at his phone.

'We'd better hurry,' Ellen urges, leading the way along the street.

Harlan sets off after her. I trudge behind them, my emotions all over the place. I get why Ellen and Harlan need to go home, but no way can I come this close to finding Asha, only to turn around and walk away.

As we reach the stop, the bus pulls up.

'Here we go,' Ellen says, sounding relieved. 'With any luck, we'll be home before the adults miss us.'

177

'Yeah, I think so,' Harlan adds. 'We should be able to get a connecting bus at—'

'I'm not getting on,' I say.

My cousins turn and look at me as a gust of wind whirls around us. The bus door opens and two elderly women sitting at the stop heave themselves up and shuffle towards it.

'Willow, you heard the guy on *The Cutter*. He won't take you. Anyway, you can't stay here on your own,' Ellen protests.

'Yes, I can,' I say, jutting out my chin.

The two ladies are climbing on board now. Harlan gazes anxiously after them. I can tell he's worrying that the driver won't wait for us.

Ellen puts her foot on the bottom step, then turns and says, 'Willow, this is mad, you—'

'I'll sneak on board the boat once it's dark,' I say. 'If I hide well enough, they'll end up taking me without realizing.'

'Stow away?' Harlan's jaw drops. 'Are you serious?'

The bus driver leans out and barks, 'On or off?' He points to Ellen's foot, still occupying the bottom step.

She hesitates.

'Go,' I urge. 'I'll be fine. It's what I need to do.'

A tiny pause; then Ellen nods. 'Okay, Willow,' she says. 'Good luck!'

'Yeah, good luck, cuz!' Harlan mutters.

They climb on board and show the driver their tickets. The bus grumbles into life and pulls away. As it disappears up the street, I catch sight of my cousins' faces pressed against the back window, looking out at me. A light drizzle starts to fall. I raise my hand and we wave at each other until they are out of sight.

I am alone.

As I scurry back to the harbour, the misty rain stops and the sun comes out. I try to take this as a good omen, but the truth is that I'm so terrified, I'm actually shaking. What was I thinking, insisting on staying here by myself? How am I going to carry out my plan to stow away on board *The Cutter*? And what on earth am I going to do once I get to Dimity Island?

I have barely any money and no idea what the people on the island have done to Asha. I take a deep breath. I'll just have to work it out as I go.

I reach the harbour and look across the water towards the boat at the end of the jetty opposite. Kieran is still working on deck, so there's no point trying to sneak on board now. The two men sitting in front of the tackle shop have gone, so I scuttle over there, then creep around to the back of the shop. Some industrial bins are lined up under an overhanging bit of roof. I settle myself between the wall and one of the bins and examine the contents of my bag: two ham rolls left over from the batch Ellen blagged for us earlier, plus my phone, a bottle of water, a thick jumper and a lip gloss – shoved in the bag in the hope that I'd have time to make myself look as good as possible before finding Asha.

I nibble at half a roll. I'll need to save my supplies. I'm not really that hungry anyway. I'm too preoccupied wondering how I'm going to get onto *The Cutter* and find a place to hide. Then I put on my jumper, shove everything else – apart from my phone – back in my bag and check my battery. The waterproof cover I brought is also a charger but, even so, I'm not sure it will last me all the way through tomorrow. I switch it off, then immediately turn it on again. I need to send Dad my next message:

Staying over at Mandeep's, if that's okay. We can carry on working on the project in the morning. Thanks. Love you, W x

I read through what I've written and delete the *love you*. It's not that I *don't* love Dad. Of course I do. But it's

180

hardly my normal way of signing off a text, and I don't want him getting suspicious and calling Mandeep's mum to check on me.

An hour passes and the light starts to fade. Gulls screech overhead, swooping down and pecking at the litter on the ground in front of me. A man comes out to dump some rubbish in the bin. He glances at me dismissively and I tense up, certain he's going to tell me to get lost, but, instead, he just mutters something under his breath and – without making eye contact – hurries away as if he wants to forget I'm there.

I wait five minutes to make sure he's gone, then creep around to the front of the shop. The harbour is dark now, with just one street lamp at the end of the stone jetty and the low moon clouded over, casting a moody, murky light across the water. *The Cutter* is in darkness, no sign of Kieran. I head towards it. A man and a woman are on the deck of one of the boats that I pass, busy with brushes and cloths. Thankfully, neither of them pays me any attention as I attempt to stroll nonchalantly past.

Beside the water, without the heat of the sun, the air is cool and I hug my jacket tight around me as I walk. I reach the boat, stop and look around. I can't see anyone from here, which, hopefully, means nobody can see me either. My heart is in my mouth as I grip the side of the hull, take a deep breath and step onto the boat. Whoa! The deck under my feet bobs and tips. I grab the rail to steady myself, my eyes darting around for a good place to hide.

I make my way cautiously to the tarp on the far side. It's already drawn over a row of boxes. There's not much room, but I crouch down, lift the flap and squeeze between two boxes marked *Rice*. I lie on my side, pressing myself against the hull of the boat, then reposition the boxes and draw the flap back over them. Hopefully it won't look like anything has been disturbed.

My heart is beating fast. Still, at least I've made it here without being spotted. It suddenly hits me again how alone I am, how terrifying this is and how worried poor Dad would be if he knew where I was and what I was doing. For a second I badly wish I really was on that sleepover with Mandeep. Then I push the feeling away. I can't stop myself being scared, but I'm determined to do this, even if it is crazy. I smile to myself. Nobody – from my protective dad to any of my friends at school – would think I'm capable of the risks I'm taking.

I can hardly believe it myself.

The deck is cold and hard underneath me. All I can see from my hiding place is a small patch of wood. I wriggle around a little, trying to get comfortable, then reach into my bag for my drink bottle. I take a sip of water and a bite of roll – I'm still not very hungry, but I need to eat to keep my strength up – then press myself back against the hull. A soft rain starts pattering on the tarpaulin over my head. I suddenly realize I'm warmer than I have been in hours, and that – combined with the soft slap and swish of the waves – makes my eyes close, though surely I'll never get to sleep.

I wake with a start. My body is numb with cold. I peer out from under the tarp, to see a thin, grey, orange-streaked light creeping over the horizon. Dawn is on its way. I don't dare stand up, so I just stretch out as much as possible. I'm starving hungry now and I wolf down the remaining food and the rest of my water.

I curl up again and let the waves lull me back to an uneasy sleep.

I wake again. This time to the thud of footsteps on the deck.

My eyes snap open. A pair of boots pass right by me. I freeze.

More footsteps; then shouting.

Thuds as additional boxes are loaded in front of me, the edge of the tarp tugged over them. My hiding place grows darker. My heart is beating fast.

'Faisal! Did you put the rice boxes on?' It's Kieran, his voice carrying across the wind.

'Dunno, I'll check,' Faisal replies.

I watch the sides of his boots as he stomps across the deck. He stops, just a metre or so away from where I'm hiding. The tarpaulin creaks as he lifts it. A moment later, he slaps it down, muttering under his breath. He takes a step closer. My stomach falls away. The rice boxes are the ones I'm hiding behind. Another footstep. Faisal is right in front of my hiding place now. His hand reaches down, feeling for the tarp.

I hold my breath.

'Ah, Faisal! I just remembered!' Kieran calls out. 'I stowed them yesterday.'

The tarp falls again and I blow out my breath.

I'm safe. At least for now.

The sun is fully up and my hiding space growing warmer, when the engine turns over and I realize we're moving.

I'm on my way to Asha's island.

The motion of the boat feels weird at first; then I just go with it. There's no chance of me sleeping again. Not only is the deck beneath me far too hard and my body aching and sore, but I quickly lose track of time and have no idea how soon we'll be arriving at Dimity Island. Nor how I'm going to get off the boat without anyone noticing.

It feels like the journey lasts for ever, but, at last, the boat slows to a gentle chug. The crew, who have been mostly silent throughout the journey, start shouting instructions to each other.

'Grab the rope!'

'Watch that rock to starboard!'

I wriggle to the edge of the tarpaulin and peer out from underneath it. Faisal and Kieran are on the other side of the small, raised cabin, their heads turned away from me towards the jetty, which looms closer with every second. I need to get off this boat.

Now!

I check my phone is still switched off and secure in its waterproof covering, then I creep out from under the tarp, leaving my backpack behind. My heart thumps against my chest as I try to move my cramped muscles. The wind blasts at my face, far fiercer than it was back in Salthaven. I peek over the hull of the boat, looking past the edge of the jetty to the coastline of the island. This is it! My heart thuds as I take in the small sandy beach with trees on either side and the two-storey brick house rising up beyond.

A tall man in an orange cap appears in the doorway of

the house. I crouch down, out of sight.

'Morning, Tem!' Faisal shouts, waving.

I freeze. Tem is Lydia's husband – the other owner of the island.

Does that mean he was one of the people who took Asha?

We're surely too far away for the man to hear Faisal's words, but he waves back. Out of the corner of my eye, I see Kieran raise his arm in response. Tem turns and goes back inside, shutting the door behind him.

Any second, the two men will turn and see me. If I get in the water now, maybe I can swim to the trees to the left of the house, then get ashore without being spotted and start my search for Asha. I give Faisal and Kieran a final, swift glance, then I slip over the rail into the water. It's shockingly cold, but I mustn't stop moving.

I take a huge breath and dive down, swimming away from the boat and towards the trees. The saltwater stings my eyes. My clothes drag, heavy and wet against my skin. My trainers are like weights. But I keep pulling at the water. Thank goodness I'm a strong swimmer. Dad took me for lessons; then I swam at least once a week after that, all through primary school. I still go to our local outside pool – I love being in the water.

This is different though. The water is *so* much colder.

And it requires all my strength to swim against the fierce current. I take stroke after stroke, my lungs burning. I need to get as far away from the boat as possible, while keeping close to the shore.

One more pull. And another. One more.

Just as my lungs feel like they're about to burst, I come up for air. As my head breaks the surface, a wave crashes over me and I splutter, water filling my mouth. I gasp, treading water. It's just open sea in front of me. Where's the shore? I spin around, desperate to find the trees. There they are, behind the beach, a row of green branches that sway in the wind. Much further away than I was expecting. I try to gather my bearings and catch my breath.

To my left I can see the tip of the jetty and *The Cutter* alongside, though the house is hidden from view now. The man in the orange cap, Tem, is on the jetty by the boat. Faisal and Kieran are still on deck. I slowly swim a little further along the coast, until I'm fully out of sight. I'm already exhausted as I turn towards the shore. I kick as hard as I can for the trees, but the current is still tugging at me, forcing me back out to sea.

It's too strong. I fight it, but my arms are heavy as stone and I'm weighed down by my clothes and shoes. I'm exhausted. I can't do it. Panic rises. The harder I try to swim to shore, the further away it seems. I stop resisting. Fighting isn't helping me get closer to shore and I'm growing more and more tired, the waves crashing relentlessly over me. I suck in deep breaths, trying to control the terror that sparks all over my body, as the water draws me along. At least I'm drifting away from the jetty; I can't see *The Cutter* any more. The waves fling me about – first closer to the curving shore on my right, then further away. I'm not just tired now – I'm frozen. My hands and feet are numb. Filmy saltwater splashes against my face and it's getting harder to haul myself up, above the waves. A minute more and I'll lose what little strength I have left.

A series of rocks rise up from the open sea in front of me. Waves lurch and crash against them, pitching me to and fro. Desperate, I reach out for a rock as I pass. I grab it, pressing my fingers against the sharp, cold stone. With a huge effort, I manage to fling both arms around it. Panting hard, I heave myself out of the water and haul myself onto the flat top of the rock. I lie there, trying to catch my breath, heavy legs dangling in the sea. Above my head, the sun rises higher in the sky, then goes behind a cloud. I'm shivering, my clothes like clamps on my body, solid with water.

I glance across to the island. Land, in the form of a

small stony-beach cove, is just a few metres away — far closer than I thought. My heart surges with hope. Maybe the current has brought me closer to the shore, or maybe the tide is turning. Either way, all I have to do is swim across this short stretch of sea and I'll be on dry land.

It's the last thing I want, but I make myself slide into the water again. At least it's warmer now against my cold skin. In fact, to my surprise, it feels good to move my stiff arms and legs. I start swimming, pulling as hard as I can. The waves catch me and propel me forward and I glide easily towards the shore. In seconds my feet are scuffing the sea bed. I stop swimming and stand up to find the water at my waist, then wade the rest of the way to the beach.

Emerging from the water, I'm dripping and shivering with cold. At least my phone is still safe in its waterproof pouch. I take in my surroundings. Beyond the little stony cove is a rough path that winds around the coast. A green, tussocky hill rises up in the distance behind it. There's no sign of either people or buildings. Which I guess isn't surprising: I know from my research that fewer than thirty people live on the island.

I decide to stay in the cover of the trees, while following the path around the island. That should give me the best chance of spotting any residents before they see me. I set off, heading left, in the opposite direction from the big

189

house and the jetty. Frozen, I hug my arms around my body. My clothes and hair are wet and heavy against my skin, and my trainers squelch with every step. At least the sun comes out. I lift my chilled face to warm my skin, then hurry along again.

I round a bend, close to the path – and come face to face with a young man in jeans and an older woman with long, silvery hair. They stop, abruptly.

I stop too.

The pair stare for a second, taking in the dripping-wet state of me. For a moment all I can think is how awful I must look.

'Hello, dear. Where on earth did you come from?' the old woman asks. She has a wrinkled, weather-beaten face and wears a long padded jacket.

The young man smiles sympathetically and hope unfurls inside me. 'I'm Aaron and this is my grandmother, Sally,' he says. 'What about you?'

I hadn't intended to give my real name straight away, but the man's kindness floors me. 'I'm Willow,' I say, unable to stop my teeth chattering.

'Hello, Willow,' says Sally. 'You look very cold. Why don't you come back to my cottage and warm up. You can tell us what happened and why you're here.'

I hesitate. The police said that everyone on the island

denied knowing Asha. So it's too risky for me to tell Sally and Aaron the truth.

'I was in a shipwreck,' I say. As soon as the words are out of my mouth, I realize how stupid they sound. 'I mean, I fell overboard and swam and swam . . . and here I am.'

Sally glances swiftly at her grandson. He looks back at her, his expression full of meaning. Neither says anything. They know I'm lying, I'm certain.

'Let's get you warm and dry, shall we?' Sally says.

Is that a fake cheeriness in her voice? I'm so desperate to be warm again, I can't tell whether I should trust her or not. I don't have a choice anyway – my whole body is now shaking uncontrollably with cold. I follow the pair into a small, clean cottage. The walls and floor are bare, made of a dark grey granite, but the colourful woollen rugs everywhere cheer the place up.

Sally leads me over to the living area, where a fire crackles in the grate. Aaron slips away, while Sally brings me a pair of sweatpants and a jumper to change into. I'm still freezing, even with the dry clothes on, so she sets me in a comfy armchair in front of the flickering flames with a blanket and a bowl of delicious soup. I sip it eagerly. I hadn't realized how hungry I was. I'm not sure what the time is, but I'm certain it must be at least 9 a.m., register-taking time at school. After a while, the school office will

191

call Dad. Guilt twists inside me. He'll be so worried – especially when he finds out I never went anywhere near Mandeep's house yesterday.

I reach for my phone, then realize it's still with my wet clothes, which are with Sally. I look across to the kitchen to where she's standing in front of the window. I can't see either my clothes or the mobile. It suddenly strikes me that her grandson, Aaron, hasn't come back from wherever he went.

I'm about to ask where both Aaron and my phone have got to, when the front door is flung open. Another woman – younger-looking than Sally, though older-looking than Dad – strides inside. Aaron is behind her.

'Oh, Lydia,' Sally says, then turns to me. 'This is Lydia Dimity. She and Tem run the island.'

I stare at her, my pulse racing. Asha referred to Lydia in our first conversation. She was one of the people who abducted her.

'Hello, Willow.' Lydia tries to smile, but I can see the tension in her green eyes.

'Hi,' I say awkwardly.

'You must be here looking for Asha.'

My stomach falls away. 'You know?' I ask shakily. 'About me and Asha?'

'More than that.' Lydia is still forcing that smile. 'I

know Asha called you and told you she lived here.'

'Right.' I'm gripped by a sense of foreboding.

'Very well.' Lydia glances at Sally, then back to me. She tilts her head on one side. 'I'm guessing you stowed away on *The Cutter* – am I right?'

I gulp, nodding.

'Very enterprising.' Lydia chuckles. 'That boat's had an exciting time lately. And did you tell anyone what you were doing? Does anyone else know you're here?'

'The police don't, if that's what you mean,' I blurt out, then regret making myself sound so vulnerable. 'But . . . but my cousins know exactly where I am and what I'm doing.'

'I see.' Lydia nods slowly. 'Well, I suppose as you've come all this way, you'd like to see Asha?'

'Yes.' I frown. Why on earth is Lydia being so helpful? Surely allowing us to meet must be the last thing she wants? 'How come you're admitting she lives here?' I ask. 'The police said everyone on the island denied it.'

Lydia sighs. 'Well, unlike the police, you've actually spoken to Asha, so there isn't much point me saying she doesn't exist, is there?' She smiles again, and this time it seems more genuine. 'Look, I understand why you want to meet your sister. I know Asha is desperate to meet you too. I'm hoping that if that happens and you can see Asha is all right on the island, then we can work out some way forward that will allow the two of you to spend some time together without threatening the freedom of the woman who has looked after Asha since she was a baby.'

I bristle.

'If you can promise me that you're at least open to keeping Asha a secret – and that you can make sure your cousins do the same – then I'm happy to take you to her right now.'

There's no way I'm ready to promise that, but it's clearly the only way I'm going to get to meet Asha.

'Okay,' I say.

'Right then.' Lydia beckons. 'Follow me.'

'Er, can I have my phone, please?' I ask. 'My dad will be worried about me.'

Sally glances at Lydia.

'Let's get you to Asha first,' Lydia says, her voice now soft and soothing. 'I'd really like you to talk to her first, before you make contact with your dad.'

'Your phone's safe and sound over there,' Sally says, indicating the drawer by the kitchen sink. 'It's not going anywhere.'

'Okay.' Still feeling uneasy, I stand up and let Sally take my soup bowl. At the open front door, I squeeze into my wet trainers, then follow Lydia outside. We make our way along the path, back in the direction I came from.

Should I make a run for it?

No. I have no idea where I am – or where I would go. Anyway, my feet are sliding around in my soggy shoes. I can barely keep up with Lydia as it is.

'Where are we going?' I ask.

'Dimity House,' Lydia explains, walking even faster. 'Asha's doing a stock check in the storeroom.' She glances sideways at me. 'Everyone here has a job within the community, even the children.' I nod. Lydia smiles again. 'Gosh, Asha really will be so excited to see you.'

My heart thunders in my chest. In a few minutes I'm actually going to meet my twin sister. I follow Lydia past the tall, green-leaved trees I came ashore near earlier. They blow and sway in the sea breeze as we round the curve in the coastal path and the big brick house comes into view, with the beach and the jetty beyond. There's no sign of *The Cutter*. It must have left already.

Lydia leads me into the house. I can hear voices on the left. Small children are laughing and calling out. I relax slightly. Surely nothing really bad can happen in such a family environment? Lydia opens a door on the right, into a kitchen. A woman is kneading dough on a floured countertop. She has fine blonde hair, wisps of which peek out from under the blue scarf wrapped around her head.

195

She looks up as we come in.

'This,' Lydia announces, 'is Willow.' There's a sudden sharpness to her voice.

The woman gasps, her hand flying to her mouth. She stares at me, as if seeing a ghost. I look down, feeling awkward.

'The storeroom is in the cellar.' Lydia walks over to what looks like a cupboard door. She opens it and flicks the light switch inside, revealing a series of stone steps.

'Asha's really down there?' I ask, my voice betraying the sudden fear I feel.

'I already told you she is.' A shard of impatience lodges in Lydia's voice. 'Don't you want to meet her?'

I hesitate. Now the moment is here, I'm baulking at the prospect. This so wasn't how I wanted to come face to face with Asha for the first time, wearing a pair of baggy, borrowed sweatpants, with no make-up and my hair all matted with salt. I don't even have the lip gloss I packed – I left it behind on the boat. Across the room, the woman in the blue scarf is still staring at me.

'Come on, Willow,' Lydia says. 'Follow me.'

She sets off down the steps. I glance anxiously over at the woman in the blue scarf as if to ask if I can trust Lydia. The woman nods, so I take a deep breath and head downstairs too.

The cellar is lit by a single light bulb that dangles from the ceiling, creating shadows that criss-cross the room. It's crammed with bits of old furniture and farm equipment – I pass a tangle of horse bridles nestling between a broken chair and a pair of fence posts. Big tins of paint and varnish stand beside the entrance to a separate room at the far end. Lydia is already over there, holding open the door.

'Asha!' she calls. 'I've brought someone to see you.'

My heart is in my mouth as I follow her into what must be the storeroom.

Shelves crammed with jars and boxes line the walls, while most of the concrete floor is covered with large hessian sacks. A long floor-to-ceiling shelving unit divides the room in half. A weird mix of scents fills my nostrils – dust and herbs and soap . As I walk past Lydia and the first few sacks, I smooth down my hair, tucking it behind my ears. Then I peer anxiously around the shelving unit.

No sign of Asha. I turn. 'There's no one—'

Across the room, the door shuts with a smart rap. Lydia is on the other side, peering at me through the small glass panel. I race over, my heart pounding, and tug at the handle.

The door is locked.

'Let me out!' A tornado of panic rises inside me. I bang on the door. '*Let me out!*'

'I'm afraid I can't do that just yet,' Lydia says calmly.

'Where's Asha?' I cry. 'You said she was here.'

But Lydia has already vanished, the sound of her footsteps echoing a brisk *tap-tap* noise as she crosses the concrete floor and goes up the stairs.

What an idiot I have been. I should never have followed her. Or given up my phone. I let out a groan, remembering how I disabled the locator app on Dad's phone and turned off the function on my own.

I stagger back and sink down onto the nearest box, a sick and terrible fear swirling inside me.

An hour passes. Maybe more. Then fresh footsteps sound on the stairs. Not Lydia, I'm certain. These feet are lighter and softer. I hurry to the storeroom door and peer through the glass panel.

The girl from the video call races across the cellar towards me.

And I forget everything else. Because it's her.

It's Asha.

She stares at me through the little window. 'Oh, Willow.'

For a second she looks just like my cousin Ellen – the same tilt of the chin; the same intense, determined expression. 'I don't have long,' she says. 'My mum told me you were here. She felt bad Lydia tricked you.'

'Your mum? You mean Rose?'

'Yes – she was in the kitchen when Lydia brought you down here.'

'Oh,' I say, remembering the fair, anxious-looking woman in the blue scarf.

'She just made an excuse to call me out of class,' Asha goes on, 'but they'll notice I'm missing soon and . . .' She trails off, staring at me as if she's trying to absorb every inch of my face.

I suddenly remember my salt-matted hair and dirty skin and the terrible, shapeless clothes I'm wearing. My cheeks burn. I *hate* that this is how Asha is seeing me for the first time.

'Does your dad know where you are?' she asks, her voice full of concern. 'Is he likely to send the police after you?'

'No,' I say. 'My cousins do – they came with me some of the way, so—' I stop, wondering how long it will take Ellen and Harlan to realize things have gone wrong and raise the alarm.

Asha stares at me. There's a wariness in her expression. I hesitate, my feelings bubbling up inside me.

'I'm so sorry the police came looking for you before,'

I say, swallowing down a sob. 'I told my dad not to call them, but he wouldn't listen. He couldn't understand why, if you wanted to escape, you cared about the people who'd been holding you prisoner.'

'I never said I was a prisoner.' Asha frowns. 'And it wasn't "people" I cared about – it was my mum, Rose. She didn't know about you or . . . or our dad, when she rescued me all those years ago.'

'She still knew you weren't hers,' I point out. 'She knew that she isn't really your mother.'

Asha puts her hand on the glass between us. 'Yes, she is.'

I don't know how to respond to that, so I look away, my emotions churning. 'Whatever happens,' I say, trying to control the shake in my voice, 'it will be worse for her, for Rose, if Dad has to come here and rescue me. You need to find a way to get both of us out of here.'

'Okay,' Asha says. 'But . . . but how?'

I turn back and put my hand on the glass on the other side from Asha's hand. I swallow down all the emotions that are roiling inside me and focus on the only practical plan I can think of.

'My phone is with that old woman,' I say. 'Sally something-or-other . . .'

'Sally Brickman?'

'Yes. She found me when I came ashore,' I explain. 'She's got my mobile in her kitchen drawer – the one by the sink. You have to get it and call Dad. The pass code is zero, one, zero, six.'

In the distance, Lydia's brisk footsteps – and another, heavier, tread – sound on the stairs. Asha's eyes widen with alarm.

'*Please*,' I hiss.

Asha backs away into the shadows as Lydia swoops into view, Tem at her side. Tem tips his orange cap back and squints at me through the glass. He has deep frown lines on his forehead.

'Are you sure about this, Lydia?' he asks.

I peer past them, into the cellar. Is Asha hiding? I can't see her.

'Of course I'm sure.' Lydia shoots Tem an irritated glance.

Over their shoulders I spot a tiny movement, then Asha's silhouette as she creeps out of her hiding place. A second later she disappears up the stairs.

'What are you sure about, Lydia? What do you mean?' I talk loudly, in the hope that my voice will drown out the soft pad of Asha's footsteps.

Ignoring me, Lydia glances at Tem again. 'We do it tonight, once it's dark.'

My guts twist into a knot. 'Do what tonight?' I demand. 'You'll do *what* when it's dark?' Something terrible is hidden behind their words. I can feel it. At least Asha should be upstairs and safe by now.

Lydia turns to me at last. 'We're discussing when the best time would be for your departure from this island,' she says smoothly.

ASHA

I rush through the kitchen, out of the back door and onto the beach. The cold sea air blasts my face; the taste of salt nips at my lips. The sun has disappeared behind a cloud and the waves past the jetty are crashing against each other.

Thank goodness I got out of the basement before Lydia or Tem saw me.

I take a few deep breaths, trying to get my head around what just happened. Willow is here. And I've met her. My twin sister in the flesh.

It was the weirdest thing and yet, somehow, the most natural as well.

She didn't get how I feel about Rose at all. She looked shocked when I said I think of her as my mother. Rose is Mum. Why is that so hard for her to understand? Well, there's no time to think about it now. I have to work out how to get Willow and myself off the island. And I want to meet my dad.

Except . . . if I go with Willow to the mainland, then

Mum will almost certainly be arrested for abducting me. After all, if Willow doesn't understand why I don't want her to go to prison, how can I expect anyone on the mainland to do so?

It's such a mess.

A white-hot fury rises inside me. I stand on the beach and scream into the wind. The air catches the sound and whisks it away from me.

Like everything, I think. *Everything* gets taken away from me.

'Asha!' It's Mum. She must have seen me racing outside and is hurrying over, panting for breath. 'Why are you so upset? What is it?'

I stare at her. 'Are you serious?' I cry. 'Willow is locked up and I can't see her. I have a father and I can't see him. And if I do find a way to be with them, then you'll end up in jail—' I stop, my breath catching in my throat.

Mum's face falls. 'I know.' She fingers her necklace. 'But Lydia insists we need to keep Willow's presence a secret so that—'

'I don't *care* what Lydia says!' I yell over the noise of the wind. 'What about what *I'm* saying?'

Mum stares at me helplessly. 'I just want to protect you. I *love* you.'

'Not as much as you love doing what Lydia tells you.'

The shout goes out of me, a horrible sense of desolation taking the place of my anger. 'Leave me alone!' I tear away, running along the beach, then around Dimity House. As I reach the path that winds around the island, I glance over my shoulder. At least Mum is no longer following me.

In that moment, my decision is made: I'm going to get Willow's phone and call our dad, like Willow wanted me to.

I follow the path for a minute, then veer off it and make my way along the coast to Sally Brickman's cottage. I can see her working in her garden out the back, but instead of calling out, I scurry to the front door and open it, careful to keep out of sight. Willow said her mobile was in the drawer by the kitchen sink. I race over and pull it open. *There.* The phone blazes into life as I pick it up. The screen shows a picture of Willow, her eyes looking coyly up at the camera. It's the same sort of picture as the one on her NatterSnap profile. Now I've seen her properly, I can see it's like a weird mask of her face – definitely her, but with fuller lips, rounder eyes and bigger, shinier hair. Why does she have this version of herself on her screen? She looks so much better in real life.

There's no button to press on the front of this phone like there was with Lydia's. I feel around the side of it.

Nothing. Remembering something Silas once said, I try swiping across the screen. *Yes*, I'm in. Except . . . now the phone is asking for Face ID, whatever that is, or a passcode. I input the numbers Willow whispered to me earlier: 0 1 0 6.

The mobile opens. Where will I find our dad's phone number? Panic rises as I scroll down the screen. What should I look for? At the top right of the phone a small red lozenge flashes at me. The screen is saying the battery is low, asking if I want to go into 'power-saving mode'. Across the room, the front door gives a creak. I look up guiltily, expecting to see Sally Brickman.

But it's Mum who walks in. She must have followed me here after all.

I jut out my jaw and hold up the phone. 'I'm going to call my dad. I have a right to know him. *And* to know Willow.'

Mum presses her lips together. I swear if she starts crying again – or telling me how Lydia sees it all differently – I'm going to lose it. But instead – to my astonishment – she nods.

'Yes,' she says. 'You do have that right.'

I suck in a shuddering breath.

'I'm so sorry, Asha,' Mum goes on. 'I've been a coward. After rescuing you off those rocks twelve years ago, I let

206

Lydia call the shots, going along with everything she said because I so badly wanted to keep you. I should have taken more responsibility from the start.'

I frown. 'What are you saying?'

Mum smiles sadly. 'I'm saying that you were right earlier. I think you *should* call your father now. Get help for Willow. Leave with her. Go to him.' She pauses. 'Whatever the consequences for me.'

We look at each other. My heart thuds painfully in my chest. 'Are you sure?'

Mum nods. 'It's time I take the responsibility I shirked twelve years ago, so I can be a mother to you in the open.'

'Even if it means going against what Lydia says?'

'I have to,' Mum says. 'I can't let her hurt your sister.'

'Hurt Willow?' My stomach contracts. 'What do you mean?'

'Lydia and Tem are planning to make it look like Willow stole their motorboat and tried to get back to the mainland,' Mum says. 'But in reality they're going to set her adrift in it, to give them time to get away.'

It's like I've been punched. 'But she could die!' I exclaim.

'I know. That's why I'm going to try and stop them.' Mum takes the silver necklace from around her neck. 'I want you to have this, Asha.' She lays the little crescent moon and its shiny chain in my hand.

207

'But—'

'It's just in case something happens to me. Anyway, once your dad arrives, I probably won't get another chance to speak to you.' She closes my fingers around the cool metal.

A chill sweeps through me. 'Mum?'

'Now call your dad and get him to come here and get you and Willow off this island.'

My head reels as I turn the screen of the mobile to face me.

But the screen is black. The phone is out of battery.

Our only way of contacting the mainland is gone. I look up at Mum and shake my head. Her face drains of colour, horror in her eyes.

'We're on our own,' I say grimly.

WILLOW

I spend the afternoon pacing across the concrete floor of the storeroom. The more I think about it, the more certain I am that Lydia doesn't just want me off the island; she wants me dead. Anyone capable of stealing Asha and keeping her hidden from the world for twelve years is not going to think twice about getting rid of me.

I need to find a way out of here. But how? Hours have passed since I gave Asha the code to my phone. Yet nothing has changed. I haven't seen my sister again – nor had any sign that someone is coming to rescue me. I'm trying to stay hopeful, but it doesn't look good: either Asha hasn't tried to find and use my mobile – or she's been prevented.

There's a bottle of water in the corner that I drink from, and I find a pack of crackers and a tin of sardines in the boxes. I'm trying to keep my strength up. I'll probably only get one chance to run when Lydia comes for me tonight. I have to make it count.

But where will you go? The voice in my head is relentless:

pricking me with questions, reminding me what an idiot I've been to get into this mess. I'm so terrified, my hands won't stop shaking and my palms are all clammy.

It gets dark outside and the storeroom grows gloomy. I flick the switch for the electric light, which flickers a little before coming on; then I sink back onto my crate. Poor Dad will be beside himself by now. If Lydia succeeds in killing me, he'll have another missing daughter, presumed dead, just like Asha. Meanwhile, Lydia will get the islanders to cover up my death, just like they covered up Asha being here.

Lydia will get away with my murder – and Asha will be trapped here for years more.

Footsteps tap across the floor outside. I jump up as Lydia opens the door. She chucks my original clothes at me, now mostly dry.

'Change back into these,' she barks, 'then come upstairs.'

'Why?' I demand. 'Where are you taking me?'

But Lydia has already disappeared.

I put on my joggers, top and jacket, which is still damp, then walk out, climbing the stairs from the cellar into the kitchen. Lydia is waiting by the back door, Tem at her side. I look hard at Tem. He's avoiding my gaze, his orange cap pulled low over his eyes as he shifts awkwardly from side to side.

A pinprick of hope thrills through me. Maybe he won't be able to go through with killing me.

'Come on,' Lydia orders.

Tem shrugs, then turns up his collar. 'Okay then.'

My heart sinks. No way is Tem going to stand up to her. Of course he isn't. He's gone along with everything ever since I arrived. He might not be happy that I'm going to end up dead, but he'd rather that than risk his wife going to jail.

The three of us make our way out of the back door. The roar of the sea and the whoosh of the wind fill my ears. The chilly air drives through me and I zip my jacket up to the neck. The moon is out, three-quarters full and shining brightly in a clear night sky. It casts a stream of light across the coastal path. Lydia sets off along it. I follow, with Tem close behind. Too close for me to try running away.

We walk for several minutes in silence – I can't make out much, but we pass a few cottages with their windows alight, like eyes, I think, watching me walk past. Except, of course, no one will be watching. And, even if they are, they'll buy into whatever lies Lydia tells them. One of the first houses we pass is Sally's. I peer anxiously towards it, hoping to spot her hovering at one of the windows. But there's no sign.

On we walk, passing more cottages. Is one of these

where Asha lives, with Rose? I strain my eyes, looking out for my sister. Where is she? We stop before the coast rises into jagged rocks and then we turn off the path. Tem and Lydia take out torches and their light bumps over the uneven ground. Ahead of us is some sort of metal cage. The torchlight glints off a huge padlock on the side nearest to us. Inside the cage is a motorboat, about a quarter of the size of *The Cutter*. As we draw closer I can see that two sides of the cage descend into the water. The motorboat bobs on the water inside, attached by a rope to a post on dry land.

As we reach it, Tem unlocks the cage, unfolding it back on itself so that the vessel has free access to the open water.

'In there,' Lydia orders, pointing to the motorboat. She takes a small key out of her pocket.

'I'll fetch the petrol,' Tem mutters. 'It needs a top-up.'

A shiver snakes down my spine. This is my chance. While Tem is distracted, I can make a run for it. But, as Tem steps towards a large box set back from the shore, Lydia grips my arm.

'Don't think about running,' she says softly, her words all the more menacing for being spoken so quietly. 'You've got nowhere to go, anyway.'

I start shaking, a fresh terror ricocheting around my head. I can't think straight, but I have to. It suddenly strikes me how ridiculous I've been – I came here to save Asha and now I must save myself. I have to do something. Get away from Tem and Lydia.

Anything but get on that boat.

I swallow hard, fear weakening my legs. I've never been so scared in my life. Lydia is yanking on my arm, tugging me towards the boat. I pull away, but she just grips me tighter.

'Let go!' I yell.

A second later, Tem is back, the petrol can in his hand. He puts it down to help Lydia drag me into the boat. I kick out at them with my legs.

'Let me *go!*'

'For pity's sake, Willow,' Lydia snaps. 'I'm trying to be civilized here, but if you don't calm down, I'll tie your hands and feet.'

I stop struggling. Clearly, there's no way I can stop them getting me into the boat. I need to save my strength for what's ahead. Maybe I can jump out once we're a little way from shore, then swim back to the island.

They'll only find you again, says the voice in my head.

Yes, I think. *But it's better than doing nothing.*

I let Tem and Lydia shove me onto the boat. Lydia orders me to sit on the narrow seat along the side. She unties the rope from its post, then stands on the rocky

213

ground holding it, while Tem bends down for the petrol.

I lean forward, heart thumping, my head in my hands.

'Aaaagh!' A high-pitched scream erupts from behind a large rock to the left. My head jerks up. 'Aaaagh!'

Tem stops in his tracks. Lydia tenses, peering into the darkness. Out of the gloom, a small, dark object flies through the air. It hits Lydia on the side. 'Ow!' she shouts.

Another object flies at her. Is it a stone? This one just misses her thigh. Tem is running in the direction of the thrower. A third shot hits Lydia sharply on her shoulder.

'Aah!' She shrieks in pain, dropping the rope. She clutches her arm, the key to the boat dangling from her fingers as she stares into the gloom.

Behind her, a dark shape races out of the shadows. It's Asha! In a split second she's run past Lydia, grabbed the key from her hand and flung herself into the boat. As Asha flies past me to the stern, Lydia steps forward to pick up the rope – but the boat's engine is already roaring into life, Asha's hand on the tiller. With a jerk, we lurch backwards. Water splashes in over the side. I grab the gunwale.

'*Stop!*' Lydia screams after us. 'Come back!'

But the island is already receding, the dark sea looming ahead. Asha, her hand still gripping the tiller, turns the boat. An expression of intense concentration is on her face as she powers us forward, into the night.

ASHA

I can't see a thing up ahead, apart from the frothy tips of the rolling waves. The distant sea is dark and choppy, and the moon – which shone so clearly just a few minutes ago – is shrouded by clouds. The wind and spray blast against my face. I glance back at Willow. She's glued to her seat, her mouth open in shock. Even in the gloom of the night, I can see that she's gripping the gunwale so tightly, her knuckles are white.

'Are you all right?' I ask.

'Will they follow us?'

'No,' I say. 'The only other boats on the island are too slow – they'd never catch us.'

'Right.' Willow is shaking. 'They . . . Lydia and Tem . . . I was sure they were going to kill me . . .'

'They were planning to abandon you at sea.' I grimace. 'Mum – Rose – told me everything.' I check the dark vista ahead of me again. I've only been out in this motorboat a few times, and steering it through the rolling sea at night is far harder than I was expecting. It strikes me that this

215

is probably the same boat that brought me to the island twelve years ago. The thought reminds me of Mum – and her agonized face as she apologized earlier this evening.

'I tried to call our dad,' I say, pushing down the raw hurt that rises inside me, 'but your phone has stopped working.' I take it out of my pocket and pass it to her. 'I think it ran out of the battery thing.'

Willow takes the mobile and stares down at the blank screen, a dazed expression on her face.

I touch Rose's silver-moon necklace, now fastened around my neck. A lump lodges itself in my throat. 'Mum did a terrible thing in stealing me,' I say, as the wind drops. 'She should have made more effort to find out if I had a family, not just rely on what Lydia told her. But she's always loved me like I was her own and . . .' I hesitate. 'And tonight she's started trying to make up for everything she's done wrong. It was her idea to throw those potatoes to distract Lydia and Tem so we could escape.'

'Potatoes?' Willow echoes blankly.

'Yes. We knew they'd take you in this boat so I kept watch behind the storage box, where I hid when the police came. I waited and waited.' I pause for breath. 'I don't know exactly what I'd have done if it hadn't worked out like it did, but . . . here we are. On the way to your dad.'

Willow meets my gaze. 'Asha . . . ?'

216

'Yes?' I'm expecting her to ask more about Mum, but instead she just says:

'He's *our* dad.'

'Of course,' I say. 'I know. I want to meet him.'

'You really do?' Willow looks out to the sea all around us, as if she's taking in our surroundings for the first time. Her voice is fragile, like a twig that might break at any second. 'Where exactly are we going?'

'To a beach just south of Salthaven, on the mainland,' I say. Then I add, trying to sound reassuring, 'It's not that far. A few hours. So long as we keep heading away from the island in a straight line, we should be fine.'

Willow nods and visibly relaxes a little.

'Once we reach land, we'll find a phone and call . . . our dad, okay?'

'Okay.' She sits back. 'That sounds good.'

'Hopefully, once we're there, I'll be able to get help for Mum. For Rose. To try and make everyone understand how manipulated she's been.'

Willow doesn't react. I'm not sure she's even listening.

A distant rumble growls across the sky, loud and threatening. The air grows even cooler. I've lived on the island long enough to recognize the signs: a storm is definitely coming – and soon.

'Was that thunder?' Willow shivers.

I nod, hoping that my anxiety isn't showing on my face. 'I'm sure we'll make it to the mainland before it gets really bad.'

'But the supply boat, *The Cutter*, took just over two hours, and this boat isn't going as fast.'

Another rumble of thunder sounds. I press down hard on the tiller, urging the boat on. Speckles of rain land, lightly, on our faces, mixing with the sea spray. Trying to distract Willow from the threat we're now facing, I take out the wool hats I stuffed into my pockets earlier. Mum knitted these for me last winter. As I stare at them, fear for her safety washes over me again. Where is she now? I wish I knew. Did Tem and Lydia catch her? Will they hurt her?

I chuck the hats to Willow. 'Here,' I say. 'Take one.'

And what will happen once I've been reunited with my dad? Will he argue for me to live with him, not Mum? Will she go to prison?

Will I ever see her again?

'What are you thinking about?' Willow asks, looking up from the hat she's twisting in her hands.

'My mum.'

Willow frowns. 'You mean Rose?'

I nod.

'I get that she *feels* like your mum,' Willow says, 'but she still stole you.'

I stare at her. The rain falls more heavily, pattering down on the boat. 'Didn't you hear what I told you earlier?' I ask. 'She's always loved me like—'

'It's not love to be selfish.' There's a raw sharpness to Willow's voice. 'She's kept you a prisoner on that awful island for twelve years.' Her words are like acid.

'She just risked her life to help us escape.'

Willow says nothing.

Tears prick at my eyes. Blinking them back, I clear my throat, then say, 'Are you going to take one of those hats, or what?'

Willow examines them, holding each one up in turn. There's not much to choose between them: one is knitted from thick grey wool patterned with snowflakes, designed to keep out the winter cold; the other is a sludgy blue and made from finer wool, aimed at keeping out strong spring winds.

Neither will offer much protection against the driving rain.

Willow's hand hovers over them both as she carries on peering closely at them. I stare at her, bemused, wondering what on earth she's debating.

She finally takes the blue. 'I think this will suit me best,' she says.

I give a scornful laugh. 'We're on a boat in the middle

of the sea with a storm coming, and you're worried about how you look?'

Willow shrinks back, the hat in her hand. She looks down at her feet. The bit of her face that I can see is flushed. 'I just don't look nice in hats,' she says at last.

This strikes me as possibly the stupidest thing I've ever heard. 'What does looking nice have to do with wearing one?' I ask.

'It's just how it is.' Willow shrugs. 'I've never even posted a picture wearing one.'

I think back to the picture of her on her phone. 'Well, you look weird in your pictures anyway. Like that one on your phone? You look much nicer in real life . . . you know, more natural . . . prettier . . .'

Willow looks up, her forehead creased in a frown. 'But everyone uses filters. We all look way better with them.'

I'm not sure what filters are and I've clearly said something that doesn't make any sense to her, so, instead of replying and getting slapped down again, I check the sea ahead. The moon is covered in cloud and it's hard to see more than a few metres in front of us. The boat is rocking more violently too, while the raindrops are bigger and heavier. I pull on the grey hat, tucking my hair inside it, then draw up the hood on my jacket.

We motor on in silence.

Twenty more minutes pass. The thunder stops, but the rain gets steadily stronger and the wind whips up the waves, which are now buffeting the boat from all directions.

'This is bad, isn't it?' Willow asks. She's put her hat on now, tucking her hair into it like I did. 'How much longer till we get to shore?'

'A while,' I say vaguely. The truth is, I'm no longer sure if I'm even still steering us away from the island. The rain is sleeting down, driving against my face like needles. I'm not wet anywhere else, thanks to my waterproofs, though I can see poor Willow is already soaked. But my hands are freezing. I reach inside my waterproof jacket and feel for Rose's little crescent moon. The touch of the metal, warm against my skin, makes me feel stronger.

Maybe we can do this, after all.

And then the engine splutters. Gives a *pfft* noise. And stops.

I stare at the tank below the tiller in horror.

'What's happening?' Willow asks, her voice rising in panic.

It's the worst possible thing – at the worst possible time – and in the worst possible weather.

'We've run out of petrol.' I can't control the petrified shake in my voice.

221

'What . . . what does that mean?' Willow stares at me, eyes wide with fear.

'It means,' I say, 'that we're going to have to row.'

WILLOW

Is Asha serious?

'Row?' I splutter. 'I've never rowed a boat in my life!' I'm already wet through. My jacket is drenched and the hideous woolly hat Asha offered me is damp against my head. 'Going all the way to the mainland will take *hours*. And there's this storm.' I wave my hand, indicating the tumbling waves and pouring rain around us. I wipe the spray off my face. 'How are we going to row in this?'

Asha stiffens. 'Well, I'm all ears if you have a better suggestion.'

I shrink back into my hard wooden seat. She doesn't need to be rude. It's all right for her – she's used to living by the sea. She's probably been out on boats every day since she came here. Plus, unlike me, she's almost certainly nice and dry inside her big, properly waterproof jacket.

'Come on.' Asha picks her way carefully along the boat to the seat that goes across the middle, from one side to the other. She indicates the oars that are stored one on each side of the boat. I take mine out – it has a long handle

223

with a paddle at the end and is heavier than I'm expecting. I grunt as I heave it over the side of the boat and place it in the water.

'Through the rowlock, there.' Asha shows me how to place the handle in a semi-circular bit of metal on the side of the boat. 'That'll stop the oar sliding away.'

The paddle of my oar now in the water, I grip the end of the handle with both hands and give it a tug. The boat shifts a little sideways.

'Wait a sec.' Asha is busy fitting her own oar. 'We have to work together. Okay, I'll count us in,' she orders. 'Then we need to move at the same time, with the same effort level. Otherwise we'll go in circles. Oh, and don't put the oar in too deep.'

We get started. It's hopeless. Whereas Asha is able to pull the boat successfully forward, I can barely shift it an inch. The rain is coming down steadily now, in thick, relentless sheets. My clothes are cold and heavy and I'm beyond tired. It feels like I haven't slept in a week.

'You have to work harder, use your whole body, not just the arms,' Asha insists. She's having to shout now over the pouring rain.

'Maybe you could work *less* hard,' I suggest loudly. 'In case you hadn't noticed, I'm weak as well as ugly.'

Asha stares at me from under the hood of her

waterproof. Her dark eyes spark with life and energy and her perfectly oval face glows like she's got on the world's best-ever moisturizer. 'You're not ugly!' she shouts over the storm. 'Or weak.'

I turn away. Easy for her to say, when she's so effortlessly perfect. I pull hard on the oar, putting my whole body behind the stroke like Asha suggested. To my surprise, it works. The boat moves further, and it's actually less effort.

'Good, that's much—!' The end of Asha's sentence is lost as the wind whips up suddenly, driving the rain like knives into our faces.

The boat rises, then drops on the mad, crashing waves. We attempt a few more strokes; then Asha puts her hand over mine.

'It's no good!' she yells over the wind. 'We need to stop and bale out.'

I look down. I hadn't even noticed, but the bottom of the boat is already covered with the seawater that has splashed in from all sides.

Asha cups her hands and scoops out a palmful of water.

'Help me!' she shouts.

As we work side by side, I notice the boat is spinning slowly around in the sea. 'Which way is the mainland?' I yell, stopping my baling for a moment.

'No idea!' Asha doesn't look up.

My heart lurches into my mouth. 'You mean we might be drifting back to the island?'

She nods.

Great. I keep scooping out water as the storm rages around me. This is all such a disaster. I came to rescue Asha but then she had to rescue me, and now *both* of us are in trouble. Dad will be terrified – and furious. And nothing is like I thought it would be – I imagined meeting my twin sister would feel comfortable and safe, like coming home. But the truth is, Asha and I don't get each other at all. All that nonsense she came out with earlier, about Rose. I don't understand how she can think of her as her mum, let alone believe that keeping her clothed and fed makes up for ripping her away from her old life.

It feels like Asha doesn't even care that much that we were separated – after I came all the way to the island to find her. And now, on top of all that, we're trapped in this useless boat on this terrifying sea in this pouring rain.

Wham!

A huge wave slams against the boat. We're thrown sideways. My arm bangs, hard, against the hull.

'Aaagh!' I cry out.

'Are you okay?' I can barely hear Asha as the storm tosses the boat up and down and side to side. It's like we're in one of those sick-making funfair rides, but with rain and seawater lashing at us from all directions.

'Move!' Asha yells, scrabbling into the bottom of the boat and gripping the middle seat hard. 'Hold on!'

I scramble down. We kneel side by side, clinging on for dear life. I close my eyes, putting every ounce of energy into not letting go of the wood. My frozen fingers can barely hold on – then I feel something strong and warm pressing down on my right hand. I look up, as Asha's fingers curl around mine.

As if giving up in response to our show of togetherness, the waves rise half-heartedly then slap back into the sea. The water subsides and the boat steadies a little. A moment later, the rain softens to a gentle patter and then stops.

We sit back, exhausted.

'Should we try rowing again?' I ask.

Asha looks up at the sky. The clouds are scudding across the moon. 'When I can see the stars a bit better. They'll help guide us to the mainland. Let's just catch our breath for a minute.'

I nod, leaning back against the hull of the boat. I'm still shivering with cold, but at least the driving wind and rain has gone.

A roar sounds overhead, making us both jump. A bright white light appears above us in the sky.

Asha's voice rises. 'What's that?'

ASHA

Light fills the sky. I close my eyes tight, suddenly terrified. The storm might have subsided, but the noise from above is, if anything, greater than before. The huge growling rumble batters my ears as fresh waves are churned up, splashing spray on my face. The boat rocks violently.

'It's a helicopter!' Willow shouts.

I look up, shielding my eyes from the glare. Yes! There, high above us, silhouetted against the grey night clouds, a helicopter is whirring. Apart from one or two that flew close to the island over the years, I've only ever seen them in pictures. As the two of us stare upward, a man leans out from the opening. He's wearing a harness attached to a rope. He gives us a short, brisk wave, then starts descending towards the boat.

'He's coming for us!' Willow shrieks.

We watch the man get lower and lower. The helicopter is creating a huge downdraft that swings him to and fro. The sea boils around us, rocking the boat wildly. It tips forward as the man lands inside. He crouches down, his eyes fixed on us.

'Willow? Asha?' His voice is deep and very serious.

We nod.

'I'm Dave. I'm with the coastguard rescue team.' The tense set of his mouth relaxes into a small smile. 'Let's get you off this tub.' He holds out the spare harness in his hand to Willow. 'You first, miss. You're shivering. Over here, please. Easy does it.'

Willow shuffles forward, then lets Dave strap her into the harness.

'I'll be right back for you,' he tells me. Then he signals up to the helicopter, still blasting us with wind and noise, and the two of them are jerked off the boat.

Slowly they are winched up to the helicopter. I watch every second, my heart in my mouth. As waiting hands pull Willow inside, the wind rears up again and the boat lurches dangerously from side to side. I cling on to the hull. For a moment it feels like the end of the world. I wish I was up there with Willow. And I want Rose. My mum.

Instead I'm here in the eye of the storm, totally alone.

It seems like ages but is probably only a couple of minutes before Dave is lowered down again. This time his descent is far rockier. It's not just the helicopter's downdraft; the wind is rising too. Dave is swung to and fro. He gets close to the boat – then it surges away. He yells something.

I scramble closer to the side, straining to hear. The boat tips and I scream.

Dave yells again. He's saying something about a high line, but I can't hear properly over the noise of the helicopter. Panicking, I grasp for the spare harness in his hand. The boat gives another terrifying lurch. My cold hands clutch at air.

Dave swings past once more, tantalizingly close. But – no! – he's going up. Up in the air without me.

'Wait!' Without thinking, I hurl myself towards him. My hood flies back as I grab the damp plastic straps of the spare harness in my fists. In the same moment I'm jerked up, off the boat. Suddenly I'm hovering above the sea. Waves splash at my boots. My arms are already aching from the cold. Dave reaches down and grabs my wrists. He's yelling again, but I can't hear. I squeeze my eyes shut and hang on. We rise, higher and higher. My arms feel like they are being torn from their sockets. If I let go now, I will fall into the sea. I have no strength left to fight the icy, angry waves. If I fall, I will die.

And I don't want to die. I want to cling on to this harness, to life, to the sister I have only just met.

I focus every fibre of my being on holding tight to the

straps. Dimly I'm aware of strong hands around my waist. A deep, reassuring voice:

'You're safe, Asha. You're okay.'

I'm being pulled sideways. The wind drops. Then solid ground under my body. The man's voice again:

'You can let go now, Asha. Open your eyes.'

The man is kneeling over me.

'Hi,' he says. 'I'm Hamza.'

Over his shoulder, I glimpse the dimly lit inside of the helicopter. I release my grip on the harness. My fingers are stiff. Numb.

'You gave us quite a fright there.' Hamza smiles with relief. 'Dave was trying to tell you to wait, that the wind was too strong. We were going to throw down a high line, but—'

'Never mind all that.' A woman in uniform appears at Hamza's shoulder as the helicopter rises fast, then swoops into the sky. 'Hello, Asha. I'm Nurinder.' She takes Hamza's place, then puts a huge crackling sheet of what looks like silver foil over my shoulders and pulls it tight across my chest. 'This is an emergency blanket, Asha. We need to get your body temperature up,' she explains. 'You were so brave out there. Now, I'm going to give you a moment to catch your breath, then I'll check you over. Okay?'

I nod, suddenly aware that my teeth are chattering uncontrollably. Nurinder smiles. 'What a sister you've got! Willow was yelling at you to hold on the whole way up – not that you probably heard her over all the racket. Here she is.'

Willow scrambles forward out of the shadows. For a second we stare at each other. She's wrapped in a silver-foil blanket too, her hair plastered to her head and her face white with terror. Then we fling ourselves at each other and are hugging and sobbing in a wordless embrace.

At last, I stop shaking.

WILLOW

Asha and I sit huddled together in the back seat of the helicopter. It's a bit like being on the boat, lots of rises and falls, but noisier, thanks to the engine and the whirring blades above us. I still can't take in what just happened, but Nurinder keeps murmuring, 'You're safe. You're fine . . .' as she checks our temperatures and takes our pulses.

The helicopter is packed with medical equipment stashed in neat rows. Everything is organized and calm. As the pilot flies us out of the storm and into the clear dark of the night sky, I hug my foil blanket around me, starting at last to feel warm.

'Where are we going?' Asha asks, peering through the nearest window. For the first time since we met, she sounds properly anxious. I suddenly remember that she's never been off Dimity Island before. I can't imagine how weird this must be for her.

I lean over her to look out. Down on the ground, lots of twinkling lights are scattered as far as the eye can see.

'At least we're over dry land,' I say, trying to sound reassuring.

'We're going to the helipad at Banchester General,' Nurinder says. 'The doctors there will check you both over.'

'Does my dad know that?' I ask. 'Can I speak to him?'

Beside me, Asha stiffens. Meeting Dad is going to be a huge deal for her. I reach for her hand and give it a squeeze.

Nurinder smiles. 'I'm sure someone will let your dad know you're okay once we radio in the rescue.'

I nod, feeling my body relax. Once I'm back with Dad, I'll know I'm safe.

'What about Lydia and Tem?' Asha sits bolt upright, her voice rising. 'Have the police gone after them? They were going to abandon Willow at sea – that's why we had to get away so urgently—' She stops, her eyes filling with worry.

Dave, who has been mostly silent since rescuing us, looks up from his Thermos flask cup of coffee. 'The police will come to the hospital later. You'll be able to tell them everything.'

'What about my mum?' Asha asks.

'Your mum?' Nurinder looks confused.

'She means Rose,' I mutter.

'Yes, Rose lives on the island,' Asha gabbles breathlessly.

234

'She's in terrible danger from Lydia and Tem too.'

Nurinder and Dave exchange a look. I can't tell whether they are genuinely concerned or privately signalling to each other that Asha is hysterical and talking nonsense. I look away.

'Okay,' Nurinder says in a pacifying voice. 'Now I want you girls to calm down,' she says. 'You're exhausted and you need to rest.'

'But—' Asha starts.

'Come on, now,' Nurinder urges. 'You need to conserve your energy.'

We both fall silent. Asha stares out of the window. I chew on my lip. For some reason, the closeness that I'd felt to her when we were being rescued has evaporated, like the steam off Dave's coffee. We're just too different, looking at everything from completely conflicting perspectives.

A few minutes later, the helicopter lands. Asha and I are bundled up and carried outside. The sound of people talking in low voices surrounds me. I can see bits of faces and the glare of bright electric lights. Shadows in the distance. I'm bumped along, then laid, more gently, on a trolley. A series of people check us both – asking if we banged our heads or lost consciousness. I ask to talk to the police, but the doctors want us to rest first. They insist that our official interviews can wait until morning.

I also ask when Dad will arrive at the hospital, but nobody knows. At last a nurse gives us each a pill – 'Something to help you relax,' she says. A few minutes after that, my eyes feel super heavy. I close them and let sleep overwhelm me.

When I wake again, I'm in a small, dimly lit hospital room. A nurse is fussing around me, adjusting a plastic tube connected to a needle in my arm. The sky through the window behind her is still dark.

'What's in my arm?' The words come out all croaky. I point to the needle.

'Just an IV drip.' The nurse gives the bag full of liquid above my head a brisk tap. The tube is attached to the bag. 'We needed to get some fluids into you. You were a bit dehydrated.' She gives me a kind smile.

'Where's my sister? Where's Asha?' I wriggle onto my elbows. 'She's never been off her island – she'll freak out if she wakes up all alone.'

'Don't you worry – she's just over there.'

I turn my head. There's only one other bed, a couple of metres from mine. Asha is asleep in it, her thick hair framing her face like a dark halo. The little silver moon on the chain around her neck glints in the light from the corridor.

'She woke earlier,' says the nurse. 'The doctor's given her a clean bill of health. She's just getting some sleep. How are *you* feeling, Willow?'

'Okay, I think.' I register my body, which feels surprisingly rested. 'A bit hungry, but I'm not hurt. Er, do you know where my dad is?'

'I don't, I'm afraid,' the nurse says, then smiles. 'I bet you'd like to speak to him.'

I nod eagerly, and she points to my phone. It's on the little table next to my bed, plugged into a charger.

'I thought if you're anything like my teenagers, you'd want that as soon as possible,' she says, 'so I connected it up to my own charger to be powered-up and ready for you.'

'Thank you.'

'Right, I'll leave you to it.' She turns away.

An image of Lydia's face flashes before my mind's eye. 'Wait!' I call after her. 'Are we safe here? Have the police found the people I was escaping from? Their names are Tem and Lydia Dimity.'

The nurse turns back. 'You'll be able to talk to the police in the morning.' She pats my arm. 'You don't need to worry about anything, Willow. Just get some rest. I'll be back with some toast in a jiffy.'

As soon as she's left the room, I snatch up my phone. There are loads of missed calls and messages: some from Ellen; most from Dad. I call him straight away.

'Willow?' He answers on the first ring. 'Oh, is that you? Are you all right?'

'Yes, Dad.'

'Oh, thank God. I'd given up trying your mobile – there was no . . . Anyway, it doesn't matter. All that matters is that you and Asha are all right. The police called to say you were in the hospital. They told me what you've been through. Are you really okay?'

'I'm fine.' I hesitate. 'Oh, Dad, I'm sorry I ran away. I *had* to find Asha.'

'*I'm* sorry I didn't believe you about her,' Dad says. He sounds really shaken, like I've never heard him before.

'Where are you?'

'In the car, on the way.' He pauses. 'What about Asha? Is she all right?'

'Yes, she is. She wants to meet you.'

Dad doesn't say anything for a moment, then starts explaining how worried he's been since the school called him to say I'd missed register. 'I called Mandeep's mother and when I knew you hadn't stayed the night, I contacted the police. Of course, at first they weren't interested – I got some jobsworth who kept insisting you'd probably just bunked off for the day. But a few hours later, Ellen called me. She explained how you'd all gone to Salthaven, but you'd refused to leave with them the night before and were planning to stow away on the supply boat to Dimity Island to find Asha.' He pauses again, a note of frustration creeping into his voice. 'What were you thinking, Willow? That was such a dangerous thing to do.'

'I'm sorry, Dad.'

'Ellen and Harlan were worried that you hadn't made contact.' He tuts. 'I'm angry with them too. They should have called me much sooner.'

'They were just trying to help me, Dad.'

Dad sighs. 'Anyway, I called the police again straight away and they sent someone to the island late last night, but there was no sign of you.'

'So . . . so what happened? How did you find us?'

'A woman on the island came forward and told one of the officers that you and Asha had left in a motorboat.' Dad sighs. 'Her name was Rose. She—'

'She's the one who took Asha when Mum died.'

'I know,' Dad says heavily. 'She admitted it and the police have arrested her. Whatever else she's done, she's certainly been desperately worried about you both. Just like me.' I can hear the shudder in his voice. 'I've been imagining the worst for hours. The rescue helicopter took ages to locate you and . . . you know, you've really put me through hell.'

'I know,' I say, my voice small and hollow. 'I really am sorry, Dad. When will you be here?'

'Hopefully in an hour or so,' he says.

'What about the Dimitys?' I ask. 'What did they say when the police talked to them?'

'I don't know,' Dad says. 'Willow . . . I love you.'

'Love you too, Dad.'

I put the phone down and sit back. A moment later the nurse returns with a plate of buttered toast, which I eat hungrily. As I'm finishing, another doctor arrives. She's old and wrinkly and introduces herself as Dr Lynn. She checks me over, asking more questions about the past twenty-four hours, then instructing the nurse to remove my IV line, which the nurse does.

Dr Lynn turns to leave. 'By the way, your dad has agreed you should have a DNA test so the police can confirm that Asha is definitely your sister.'

'I already know she is,' I say.

Dr Lynn nods – one of those grown-up gestures that means, *Okay, but we need actual proof.* 'Under the circumstances, we can't take Asha's DNA without a court order, but we'll do yours once your dad gets here. It's very quick and totally painless.'

240

'Okay.'

'There's some press outside,' Dr Lynn tells me. 'But don't worry. Hospital security will make sure they're kept away from you.'

'Press?' I ask.

'Local and national newspapers. There's even a TV crew. The search for you and the helicopter rescue was just on the news.'

'Oh.' I frown, glancing out of the window. The sky is still dark, though faint pink streaks are swirling through the steel-grey. Dawn can't be far away now.

'What time is it?'

Dr Lynn checks her watch. 'Almost six in the morning.' She stands up. 'Try and get some rest.'

She leaves the room and I turn on my side, watching Asha sleeping. Her shoulders rise and fall under the sheets as she breathes, deeply and evenly. A sense of relief washes over me. We got away. We're safe. And Dad will be here soon.

ASHA

I wake with a start, sitting bolt upright. My heart is racing and my eyes dart around the room, looking for the danger that surely lurks there.

But there is no danger. Just a shadowy room in a hospital. I've only ever seen hospitals in books before. Willow is in the bed by the window. She's sleeping. Lightly, I think, from the shallowness of her breath.

I wish she was awake. But then I'd have to talk, and right now I need to think. I feel like I'm rolling over and over, with no idea which way is up. I keep coming back to Mum. Where is she? How is she? Have Tem and Lydia hurt her?

What if I'm never allowed to see her again?

The phone on the little table next to Willow's bed sparks into life, filling the room with a blue glow. I get out of bed and pad over in my bare feet to pick it up. Even though I know there's no way Mum would use a mobile, even if she had access to one, I'm hoping against hope that it's some kind of message from her.

The screen shows the time – 06:17 – and the start of a message:

Please pass this text to Asha . . .

I can't see the rest without opening up Willow's phone. Which I guess I shouldn't as it's *her* phone. But then the message is for me. And it could be – it surely *must* be – from Mum. Who else would send me a message? I swipe up the screen, which asks for Face ID or a code. Face ID. Does that seriously mean the phone can open if it sees your face? Hardly able to believe it, I hold it over Willow's sleeping face. It doesn't work, so I input the four–digit code she gave me yesterday.

The full message comes on screen. It's not from Mum. It's from Silas.

Asha, hope you're ok. I saw about your escape and rescue on the news – and Rose being arrested.

I stop reading for a second, my heart lurching into my mouth. Mum's been arrested?

I'm in a house round the corner from the hospital – 33 Banchester Street. I HAVE to see you. I have evidence

243

that can help Rose. I can't come to you, but I'll wait here for one hour. Hurry! Silas.

I check the number the message was sent from – I recognize the last few digits from the letter he sent to Pixie. It's definitely his phone. But what evidence is Silas talking about? I can't think what he could have found out, but I'll do anything to try and protect Mum. I glance across at Willow. She's still asleep. There's no point me waking her. She's already made it clear that she doesn't understand why I want to help Mum.

I hurry over to the shelf beside my bed where some dry clothes have been left, neatly folded. I slip on a pair of leggings and a jumper, making as little noise as possible. Thankfully, my waterproof boots are here too, so I pull them on. I feel for the crescent moon on the necklace Mum gave me. Touching it reminds me of her, which makes me feel just a tiny bit stronger. A final glance at Willow, who is snuffling lightly in her sleep, then I grab my waterproof jacket from the hanger in the cupboard. The hanger rocks back, clicking against the sides of the cupboard. I freeze. Spin around.

Willow fidgets but doesn't wake, thank goodness.

I ease open the door and peer out into the corridor. A woman in uniform, the words *Hospital Security* on her back, is standing halfway along on the right, near the sign for the lifts. She's looking down at something in her hand. Moving as quietly as possible, I creep out of the room and turn left. I tiptoe along the corridor, give a final glance back to the security guard – who hasn't looked up – then push at the fire door at the end. I scuttle through it and on to a draughty set of concrete steps. My heart is beating wildly as I hurry down them. Everything is so big and echoey and strange.

How do people live like this, with this amount of building pressing down on them?

I'd thought the mainland would be more like our island – with houses, of course, and other buildings, but still lots of grass and trees and bushes. But all I can see through the window is a grey town full of buildings – not a green space in sight. There's a road out the front of the hospital that cars are whizzing up and down. They move *so* fast. Where are all the people in them going?

I stop at a map on the next floor down, searching for the exit. It's over by the Maternity Department, which is in a separate building in the complex. I hurry along a corridor and down another flight of stairs. I pass no one except a man with a cleaning trolley, who stares at me curiously as I speed by. In the distance I can hear someone shouting and, separately, someone crying. I shiver. I don't like it here at all.

I reach the glass doors and peer outside into the cool, grey light of dawn. A sign saying *Maternity Dept* is nailed to the wall of the brick building opposite. The hospital exit is visible beyond it. As I put my hand on the glass to push the door open, footsteps sound behind me.

WILLOW

Her hand is on the exit door.

'Asha!' I call.

She turns, startled.

'I read the message from Silas,' I say, hurrying over, my phone clutched in my hand. 'You can't go and meet him. It's too risky. We need to stay in the hospital, wait for Dad.'

'But he's got evidence that can help my mum!' Asha pleads. 'She's been arrested.'

'Then let him take it to the police himself.' The words shoot out of me. Asha recoils, eyes full of hurt. 'I'm sorry,' I say, 'but what evidence can he possibly have? You told me before, Silas hasn't been on the island for weeks. You can't even be sure the message was really from him.'

'Yes, I can – it was his number.' Asha's eyes are dark with frustration. 'You just don't want to help.'

'I do!' My voice rises angrily. 'I just snuck past that security guard upstairs to find you!'

'I'm going to Silas,' Asha insists. 'Whether you like it or not!'

She pushes the door open and strides outside. Stung, I watch her cross over the tarmac and disappear along the side of the Maternity Department. I can see the main exit beyond. A small group of men and women are huddled around it. Several have cameras slung about their necks, while at least one carries a video camera.

Asha is about to walk into a sea of journalists.

I've seen what reporters do on the news. If they recognize Asha, they'll swarm her and she'll completely freak. I hesitate for a second. It's not just the journalists. Asha doesn't have a clue how anything in the real world works. She's likely to get run over just crossing the road.

I open the doors and race after her. The dawn air is crisp and cool, the fresh morning of what will be a hot day. Asha is almost at the end of the redbrick Maternity Department when I catch up with her.

'What are you doing?' she asks grumpily.

'Helping you get to Silas,' I say. 'Though I still think it's stupid and risky. Lydia is after us. She's going to try and shut us up before we say anything against her.'

Asha stares at me for a second. 'Come on then.' She takes a step forward.

I grab her arm, pointing towards the exit. 'Not that way – we'll get harassed by all those reporters.'

'Oh.' Asha frowns.

I check my phone again. 'Anyway, that's totally the wrong way to the address Silas gave you.' I look up. 'How on earth were you planning on finding him?'

Asha shrugs. 'I was just going to ask someone.'

I shake my head, tugging her in the other direction. 'This isn't like the island. People don't just automatically know where places are.'

'Well, how will you find him then?'

I hold up my mobile. 'GPS.'

I'm certain Asha doesn't have a clue what I'm talking about, but she says nothing and lets me lead her back through the hospital and out the other side. We make our way across a section of the staff car park, then out onto a side road. I follow the map on my phone, while Asha stares all around her as we walk, her jaw open in amazement at the tall buildings and traffic.

'It's so noisy,' she says. 'And dirty.'

Banchester Street is slightly further away than Silas's message made out, but after ten minutes, we arrive. It's a rundown street. Not like Salthaven was, with its boarded-up shops and peeling paint on the doors, but full of houses with bare concrete yards out the front and tattered curtains at the windows.

'Poor Silas having to live in one of these,' Asha says.

'Who says he's living here?' I ask. 'He probably just

came when he heard you'd escaped and needed somewhere to shelter for the night.'

'I guess.'

'That's if it's really him,' I mutter.

'It *is*,' Asha insists.

'Okay, then – but *any* sign of trouble and we're out of here,' I say. 'And we only stay five minutes. Tops. My dad will be arriving at the hospital soon.'

Asha nods.

We creep up the front path of number 33. The front door isn't locked, so I push it open. The room we walk into smells damp and musty. There's no furniture, just bare walls and creaky, worn floorboards. It doesn't look like anyone has lived here for ages.

There's a kitchen area with a stained countertop to the left and another room beyond that. Stairs opposite lead up to the first floor.

'Silas?' Asha calls.

'Shh!' I hiss at her.

Above our heads, a thumping noise reverberates from the first floor.

'It's him.' Asha races over to the stairs, taking them two at a time.

'Wait!' But she's already out of sight. I follow her up the narrow staircase with a deep sense of foreboding. A dirty, threadbare carpet curls away from the grubby walls of the tiny landing. A filthy-looking bathroom is visible through an open door at one end. The other two doors, set next to each other opposite the stairs, are ajar.

Ahead of me, Asha disappears through the first door.

'Silas!' I hear her cry.

I hurry after her into a bare, unfurnished room. Sunlight seeps in through the slim gaps between the boards over the window, casting thin white streaks over the floor. Silas is sitting, hunched over in the corner. Asha flings herself at him and he hugs her.

'Oh, Asha,' he says, pulling away and pushing his dark hair off his face. 'I'm so sorry.'

Fear spirals up through my chest, into my throat. I take a step forward. Why is he sorry? I open my mouth, but before I can ask, my phone is wrenched out of my hand and I'm shoved, roughly, in the back. I stumble forward, nearly losing my footing.

As I reach the others, I spin around.

There, my phone in her hand, is Lydia.

ASHA

'Hello, girls,' Lydia says with a light sneer, pocketing Willow's phone. 'I see you got my message.'

My heart sinks as the full realization crashes over me: the text wasn't really from Silas. Nor does he have any evidence to help Mum. Willow warned me and I wouldn't listen. Instead, I've led us both into a terrible trap.

I touch my sister's arm, trying to tell her how sorry I am. Willow grips my hand. Her fingers are trembling. A hard, angry pebble lodges in the pit of my stomach.

'How did you get off the island?' I demand.

'Tem and I called in a favour,' Lydia explains. 'A friend on the mainland with a powerful motorboat.'

'But how did you know where *we* all were?' Willow asks shakily.

'We already knew where Silas was, with his uncle. As for the two of you, we just kept an ear on the police radio.' Lydia pauses. 'We won't be here long. Tem's just getting hold of some things we need – then we'll be leaving the country. For good.'

'You can't.' I say. 'What about Mum? She's been arrested.'

'That isn't my problem,' Lydia says.

'It will be when she tells the police that you helped her take Asha all those years ago,' Silas says.

'And how you locked me in a basement and planned to abandon me at sea last night,' Willow adds.

'Whatever Rose tells them will sound either like she's trying to pass the buck or flat out hysterical,' Lydia snaps.

'What about what *we* tell them?' I demand. 'Once Willow and I have explained everything you did, the police will definitely arrest you.'

'Indeed.' Lydia tilts her head to the side. 'But that can only happen *if* you're able to tell them in time. Why do you think I brought you here?'

I clutch the silver crescent moon around my neck, fear turning cartwheels through my head. 'You're going to kill us?'

'Murder *all three* of us?' Willow's voice cracks.

'You *can't*,' Silas says, horrified.

'Who said anything about murder?' Lydia says lightly. 'We're just going to leave you locked up here while Tem and I catch our flight.'

'You coward.' Contempt drips from Silas's voice.

'We always knew it might come to this,' Lydia says,

ignoring him. 'We just need a bit of time to make our final arrangements and didn't want to risk you guys talking to the police before we were done. Especially since you two have made such a fuss with the coastguard. I'm heading to the airport now.'

My heart thuds against my ribs.

'You won't get away with *any* of this,' Willow says.

'Time to go.' Lydia says. 'Goodbye.' She steps smartly back, onto the landing, and shuts the door.

Willow, rushes over to the door. She tries to turn the knob. But it just spins in her hand.

We're trapped.

WILLOW

The three of us sit down on the bare floor. Asha looks as shocked as I feel.

'How did Lydia get you here?' Asha asks Silas.

He makes a face. 'She pretended to be you, told me to meet you here. I'm guessing she did the same to you?' Asha nods numbly. 'At least you two found each other.' Silas looks over at me. 'Hi again, Willow.'

I can feel my cheeks pinking. 'Hi,' I say. 'Er, I'm sorry I was so suspicious of you when you came to my house.'

Silas smiles. 'No need to apologize. If Asha and I had been more suspicious, we wouldn't all be here now.'

Half an hour passes. Silas keeps watch by the window, in case somebody comes by and we can shout for help. Asha paces up and down the room, a look of extreme worry on her face.

'The hospital will realize we've gone,' I say. 'I'm sure the police will be looking for us.'

Neither Silas nor Asha seems comforted by this.

Another few minutes tick by. Then Asha stops by the door. She frowns.

'Do you smell that?' she asks.

Silas and I hurry over to the door and breathe in. I catch a whiff of something strong and sickly. Horror fills me.

'What is that?' Silas asks, his nose wrinkling.

'It's gas,' I explain. 'It's an old house. There must be a gas leak.'

'What does that mean?' Asha asks.

'That it will . . . That there'll be an explosion. A fire.'

Silas's eyes widen. 'We have to get out of here.'

I race across the room and push at the window, but the boards nailed over them don't budge an inch. I peer round, looking for something we could ram against them, but the room is completely empty.

Then I notice the large, square air vent set into the wall by the fireplace, just above the skirting board. 'We can get next door through there,' I suggest. 'Get out of the house that way.'

The three of us hurry over to the vent. It's screwed into position in each of its four corners, with a criss-crossing grille covering the gap. I crouch down and peer through. A matching grille dangles loosely on the other side that opens into the room next door. I examine the tiny screws holding the grille against the wall.

'If we could only undo these,' I say, 'I'm sure we could crawl through the vent into the next room.'

'I know,' Silas says. 'But we don't have a screwdriver.'

Panic rises inside me. What on earth are we going to do? And then Asha speaks – her voice filling with hope.

'What about this?'

ASHA

I hold up the silver moon on the necklace Mum gave me, showing Silas and Willow the pointed tip.

'I could use this to take off the screws,' I suggest.

'Try it!' Silas puts his arm around my shoulder, giving me an encouraging squeeze.

I crouch down in front of the metal air vent. The gas smell is horrible and I rip a strip off my shirt to wind around my nose and mouth. With fumbling fingers, I take the crescent moon off my necklace and hold its slim point to the screw in the top-right corner of the grille. It's not a perfect fit, but it's good enough.

'It's going to work,' Silas says, excited, covering his nose and mouth with his T-shirt.

I apply my trembling fingers to the little silver moon, turning it over and over.

'That's brilliant, Asha,' Willow cries. She's torn a strip of fabric off her top and is winding it over her face.

I grin; then another whiff of gas fills my nostrils. Ugh.

'You can do it.' Silas crouches down beside me, his sea-blue eyes intense.

The first screw is loosening. I finish undoing it and move to the next. The stench of gas is almost unbearable now.

'Let one of us take a turn,' Willow urges from over by the window. 'The smell is getting really bad.'

'I'm fine,' I say, though the truth is I am starting to feel a bit light-headed. 'I'm nearly done.'

I get the third screw out, then stand back, coughing, as Silas wrenches the vent back, twisting it round. With a grunt of effort, he pulls the grille off its final screw, then lies on the floor and kicks the grille opposite into the room on the other side. He scrambles up, doubling over as he coughs. The gas is overpowering.

He checks his watch again. 'Let's go.'

I squeeze through the opening into the next room. It's like the first, with bare walls and boarded-over windows. A faint hissing sound reaches me and I turn towards it. Across the room a pipe has come loose from its moorings on the wall. A crack is visible running along its side. With a jolt I realize that the soft hiss I can hear is the sound of escaping gas.

'Come on!' I shout.

Silas is already pushing himself through the air vent,

259

grunting as he twists his body to get his shoulders through. He hauls himself up. A second later, Willow follows him into the room and leaps to her feet. Hope surges inside me. Surely we're free now?

The door to the landing is ajar. I take a step towards it. And then the floor beneath me gives way and I'm falling, bits of rotten wood and dust flying around me. I open my mouth, but time slows, and before I can scream the ground rises to meet me.

I land on my ankle. Collapse to the ground, pain shooting through me. Black specks filter into the side of my vision. I look up. Through the rising dust, I can just make out Silas and Willow peering down from the room above.

'Asha!' They are both calling my name. But my head spins and I feel sick.

And then everything goes black.

WILLOW

'Asha!' I scream helplessly through the gaping hole in the floor. I catch a glimpse of her, slumped on the ground far beneath us; then the rising dust obscures her from view.

'We've got to get to her,' Silas yells. 'Move!'

I leap up. From their dark, cracked appearance, it's obvious the floorboards Asha fell through are rotten. Silas is already darting around them. I follow, fear clutching at my throat.

Down the stairs, my lungs strain for breath. My phone is lying on the kitchen countertop. I snatch it up as I fly past, then follow Silas into the next room.

My sister lies motionless on the floor. 'Asha!' I race over, my heart pounding.

She shifts, very slightly, but doesn't open her eyes. Together, Silas and I pull at her arms. She's a dead weight.

'Asha, you have to wake up!' Silas yells.

No response.

I lean closer. 'Asha!' I shout. 'Open your eyes!'

Nothing. Silas and I look at each other. A cold tendril of fear curls around my heart.

'Asha!' Silas yells.

I lean even closer. 'I am *not* leaving you. And you're sure as hell not leaving me again.' I slap her cheek lightly. 'Open your eyes. NOW!'

Asha's eyelids flutter slightly; then her eyes open.

'Come on!' Silas reaches under Asha's shoulder and hauls her up. I position myself on her other side and, together, we half drag Asha through the hall. She's hobbling, one ankle trailing behind her.

'Hurry!' Silas shouts.

We reach the front door and burst outside into the cold, fresh air. I am gasping for breath, but don't dare stop. At least there's no sign of Lydia as we carry Asha away from the house. My lungs are bursting with the effort, but we keep going until we reach the corner.

A second later, the house erupts in an explosion.

Silas and I fling ourselves over Asha, as flames and fragments fly past us. And then, as suddenly as it began, the firestorm in the street subsides. I look up, gulping in air as I lean against the crumbling wall of the nearest front yard. Now just the house is burning, tongues of fire licking high into the air. I shiver at how close we came to being trapped inside it.

Silas has propped Asha between us. I look around at her. She's watching me, a relieved smile creeping across her face, her hand touching the cheek I just slapped.

'We need to talk about your future, Willow,' she says, her voice filling with irony. 'Because if you're thinking about a job in any of the caring professions, I have to break it to you that you have zero talent for it.'

I laugh. And she laughs too. And then Silas is laughing. And the three of us hug each other as the house goes up in flames.

ASHA

Silas, Willow and I watch the house burn as Willow uses her phone to call 999, who say they're sending all the emergency services. I can put weight on my ankle now. I think it's just badly twisted rather than broken.

Once the fire brigade arrives, Willow calls our dad. He's almost at the hospital and says he will see us there. I don't know how I feel about meeting him. It's still super weird knowing that I *have* a father. I certainly can't imagine calling him 'Dad', like Willow does. But then maybe he won't want me to anyway. I mean, he thought I was dead. I guess it's going to be weird for him as well.

Will I even like him?

As Willow gets off the phone, more sirens ring through the air. Dust rises off the street as flashing lights and an ambulance comes to a screeching halt beside us. Two men in uniform – they must be paramedics – jump out. Suddenly everywhere is noise and bustle. It's overwhelming. Thankfully, Willow is explaining what happened, pointing to my ankle. Before I know what's happening, I'm being carried into the ambulance. I lose sight of the others for a moment, then they get on board too.

We don't talk much on the short journey back to hospital, except to answer the paramedics' questions. In the hospital we are separated while doctors examine us; then the police interview us. I ask the officers where Mum is, but they say they don't know. Right now, we've been ushered into a small waiting area with doors that open on to a small, private courtyard. I can't take in everything that's happening, but at least I'm with Willow and Silas again.

A police officer is stationed at the door, checking who comes in and out. We've just been told a warrant has been issued for Lydia's and Tem's arrest, though I still have no information about Mum. Silas sits near the exit, looking out for his uncle who is, apparently, on his way. Willow is perched on a chair next to him, waiting for our dad.

I hobble outside, using the stick the nurse gave me. My foot is encased in a special boot. It still aches, but not as badly as it did when I landed on it. I sit down on one of the two benches in the courtyard, opposite the small patch of grass in its centre. It's quiet out here, the air still and warm. I keep my eyes on the shiny green grass.

Footsteps approach. It's Silas.

'My uncle is here,' he says, 'so I'm going with him.' He pauses. 'I just spoke to Mum and Dad too. They'll be back in the country tomorrow. I think things will be different now. I might even go back to the island with them for the summer, like they want, before sixth form this autumn.'

I nod, too full of emotion to speak.

'Your dad's in the waiting room with Willow,' Silas says. 'He'll be out here any second.'

My dad.

'Oh.' I gulp, staring resolutely at the patch of grass. I don't want to get to the moment where we come face to face any faster than I have to.

'Are you nervous about meeting him?' Silas asks.

I shrug. *Yes, obviously.*

'Do you think he'll insist on you moving in with him?'

I say nothing, but I am certain he will. Why wouldn't he? I was stolen away from him twelve years ago. I belong to him. Even though I don't know him.

'I have to go.' Silas hesitates.

I look up at last, meeting his gaze. 'Thank you,' I say. 'For everything.'

He nods. 'See you, Asha.'

I'm left on my own. My insides twist and churn. All I can think about is what it will feel like to meet my dad. Beside me, the tap of another footstep.

I look up, expecting it to be him: my father, a stranger. But standing right there is Mum, a smile of love and relief on her face.

WILLOW

I jump up when I see Dad. He speaks briefly to the police guard at the door, then hurries inside the waiting room and scoops me into a hug. I forget everything else in the relief of having him hold me, sinking against his chest and breathing in the soft, cottony warmth of his sweatshirt.

'Oh, Willow,' he sobs, 'thank goodness you're all right.'

I lift my eyes and smile at him. Over his shoulder, Rose is scurrying past us, a policewoman beside her. I stare as they go outside to the little courtyard where Asha is sitting.

'What's *she* doing here?' I ask.

Dad sighs heavily. 'I persuaded the police to let her see Asha for a few minutes.'

My jaw drops. 'You did?' I watch as Asha flies into Rose's arms. The two of them hug each other, sobbing.

Dad puts his hand on my shoulder. 'I know it's hard to accept, but Asha's been through so much. The last thing she needs is completely to lose the only mother she's ever really known.'

I shake his hand off, feeling troubled. I can just about see where Dad is coming from, but how can it possibly be okay for Rose to carry on being Asha's mother? To get away with what she did to us all those years ago?

I go outside. Asha and Rose are still too focused on each other to notice me. I stop beside them, watching as they look at each other – at the relief on Asha's face and at the love shining from Rose's eyes.

Dad walks up beside me and puts his hand on my shoulder again and I suddenly remember how I felt when I was scared earlier, how much I wanted to be with him. Is it the same for Asha with Rose? I guess it must be.

And the difficult, complicated truth starts to settle in my head. Even if she was lied to at the time, Rose should never have torn Asha away from me and Dad all those years ago.

But that doesn't justify us ripping Asha away from Rose now.

ASHA

'Asha?'

I hear Willow say my name and I draw apart from Mum. I'm suddenly, awkwardly aware that the courtyard is now full of people. Willow is right beside us, while behind Mum stands a uniformed policewoman, two men in dark suits and a woman with a badge that says JANICE. They are all watching me carefully.

And then I notice the tall, dark-haired man hovering behind Willow. As he catches my eye, he smiles nervously and clears his throat.

'Hello, Asha,' he says hesitantly. 'Er . . . I'm your dad.'

'Hello.' I stare at him, unsure how to feel. I meet his gaze. His eyes are gentle and kind.

'It was your . . . your dad who insisted the police brought me here, before they . . .' Mum's voice cracks. 'I'm going to have to go with them now.' She takes my hand and points to the woman with the name badge. 'This is Janice Cairns – she's from social services. She's going to be looking after you for a bit.'

'No.' I grip her hand tightly. 'No! Mum, I don't want you to leave.'

'I know.' Tears spring to her eyes. 'I don't either, but . . . I'm trying to take responsibility . . . for what I did all those years ago.'

Empty inside, I watch the policewoman take Mum back through the waiting area and out of sight. For a moment I feel desperately alone, but then Willow appears at my elbow. She takes my arm and draws me onto the bench. Her touch and her voice are very gentle, as she asks, 'Are you okay?'

A lump lodges in my throat as a sense of calmness washes over me and I take Willow's hand and know that, even though my entire life has just been stood on its head, I've found my sister. My twin. And if we can face the world together, everything is going to be all right.

TEN WEEKS LATER

WILLOW

It's a scorching day in the third week of July. Dad has invited everyone on both sides of the family to our house. Lots of people want to meet Asha, and he and Rose thought that a big gathering would be the best way, without too much pressure on anyone. Asha and Rose have been here since lunchtime, helping Becky and me put up streamers and fairy lights that will make the back garden look pretty this evening.

It's not just our family we're celebrating. Last week we found out that Lydia and Tem – who were arrested and charged before they could leave the country – are selling Dimity Island to pay for their legal bills. Everyone on the island is getting together to buy it. To make up the full amount, there's a plan to crowdfund a dozen new cottages for newcomers to buy and live in.

Asha is back on the island with Rose, but she visits us every couple of weekends. She tells me that there's a new, more flexible system for running things now. There's still a load of people who want to live there off-grid, but it's fine if you don't. No judgement if people want mobiles and computers or whatever. It still sounds like the dark ages to me, but Rose says the island's back to the values it had when it was settled back in the seventies – living with tolerance and sustainability.

Rose herself isn't going to have to go to prison. This is mostly because, though Lydia kept insisting Rose had manipulated her into Asha's abduction, in the end Tem spoke up and said that it was the other way round. In order to get a shorter sentence himself, he told the truth, explaining to the police that Lydia had known all along Asha had a father and had lied to Rose from the start. She'd encouraged Rose to keep the little girl in order to get her hands on Rose's money. Tem, who is now separated from Lydia, also testified that Rose was a brilliant mother – a claim that everyone on Dimity Island backed up. It turns out that most of the islanders were in the dark about the real story.

On top of all that, I know Dad spoke up for Rose too. A lot of people think he is mad for doing that. Rose herself says he's a saint.

To me it's proof that he's a brilliant dad.

'Hey, Willow!' I look up to see Ellen and Harlan walking towards us.

Ellen's eyes are wide with curiosity as I introduce Asha. Harlan looks characteristically shy.

'Without these two, I'd never have found you,' I say to Asha.

Asha nods. 'Hi,' she says. 'Er, thank you.'

For a second everyone stands around awkwardly; then Ellen grins and opens her arms.

'Hey, cuz,' she says, pulling Asha into a hug. 'Welcome to the family.'

A minute later, she's pumping Asha with questions about everything, from her life on the island to what it was like having the DNA test, which officially proved we were twin sisters. Harlan chips in, every now and then, with a question of his own.

Asha answers them both patiently, occasionally catching my eye when a subject she doesn't want to talk about comes up – that's my cue to jump in and divert the conversation. It's funny, I know exactly what she's thinking almost all the time now, just from little looks like that. Weird that when we first met she seemed such a stranger. Now she's like the person I'm closest to in the whole world. And she says the same.

I just wish we had more time together than two weekends a month.

At last Ellen and Harlan wander off and Asha and I head to the back of the garden for a break from the onslaught of family members.

277

'You know, Ellen and Harlan really did help get me to the island,' I say to her. 'And if it wasn't for them talking to Dad, that rescue helicopter might not have got to us in time.'

Asha nods as we sit down with our backs to Dad's little garden shed, out of sight of the party. 'Ellen and Harlan were brilliant, but you were really brave.' She hesitates. 'You saved my life.'

'You saved mine.'

We look at each other.

Asha smiles. 'I was talking to Mum, and we've agreed something big.'

'What?'

'We're moving off the island. To a place near you.'

I stare at her, hardly able to believe it. 'Seriously?'

'Yeah. I'm going to start at your school in September and we'll be able to see each other whenever we want.' My heart surges with joy. Asha grins. 'It's going to be so cool being together every day. And . . . and seeing Dad more too.'

My stomach gives a little flip. That's the first time I've heard Asha call him that.

'I expect Mum'll go back to the island eventually,' she adds. 'Like, when I go to uni.'

'Hey, we could go to the *same* uni,' I say. 'Wouldn't that be amazing?'

'If there are courses we both want to do,' Asha says, then puts her hand over mine. 'But it doesn't matter if we aren't always together, because we'll always . . .' She hesitates.

'. . . be sisters,' I finish. 'Yes,' I say, smiling. 'We will.'

ACKNOWLEDGEMENTS

With huge thanks to the whole team at Simon & Schuster: Lucy Pearse, Arub Ahmed, Basia Ossowska, Veronica Lyons, Leena Lane, Laura Hough, Leanne Nulty, Dani Wilson, Dan Fricker, Jessica Dean, Eve Wersocki Morris – and also to Jodie Hodges, Molly Jamieson, Lou Kuenzler, Moira Young, Melanie Edge, Julie Mackenzie and Gaby Halberstam.

ABOUT THE AUTHOR

Sophie McKenzie is the multi-award-winning original queen of teen thrillers, whose 2005 debut, *Girl, Missing*, remains a YA bestseller. She has followed its success with two further books in the Missing series: *Sister, Missing*, *Missing Me* and many other teen thriller and romance novels, including The Medusa Project series, *Hide and Secrets* and *Truth or Dare*. Sophie's first adult novel, *Close My Eyes*, was selected for the Richard and Judy Book Club. Sophie's books have sold more than a million copies in the UK alone and are translated and sold all over the world. She lives in North London.

www.sophiemckenziebooks.com
Instagram @sophiemckenziebooks
Twitter @sophiemckenzie_

DISCOVER MORE FROM THE BESTSELLING QUEEN OF TEEN THRILLERS.